Charles D. Bell

Songs In The Twilight

Charles D. Bell

Songs In The Twilight

ISBN/EAN: 9783742814463

Manufactured in Europe, USA, Canada, Australia, Japa

Cover: Foto ©Andreas Hilbeck / pixelio.de

Manufactured and distributed by brebook publishing software
(www.brebook.com)

Charles D. Bell

Songs In The Twilight

SONGS IN THE TWILIGHT.

BY THE

REV. CHARLES D. BELL, D.D.

RECTOR OF CHELTENHAM, AND HONORARY CANON OF CARLISLE;
AUTHOR OF "VOICES FROM THE LAKES, AND OTHER POEMS,"
"HILLS THAT BRING PEACE,"
"NIGHT SCENES OF THE BIBLE," ETC. ETC.

LONDON:
JAMES NISBET & CO., 21 BERNERS STREET.
MDCCCLXXXI.

CONTENTS.

——o——

		PAGE
THE TWILIGHT	. . . .	. 3
LOVE'S QUESTIONINGS	. . . . .	. 7
EFFIE	. . . .	. 10
ONE LOOK	. . . .	. 16
MAY	. . . .	. 18
A SOLDIER'S STORY	. . . . .	. 21
WAR TIME	. . . . . .	. 26
THE SUMMERS OF THE LONG AGO	. . .	. 40
LIFE'S CONTRASTS	. . . . .	. 42

SONNETS—

REFLECTIONS	. . .	.	. 51
THE LAKE COUNTRY	. .	.	. 53
PAST AND PRESENT	. .	.	. 55
NIAGARA	. . .	.	. 58
THE HORSE-SHOE FALLS	.	.	. 60
LIFE	. . . .		. 62
DEATH	. . . .		. 63
" PER ANGUSTA AD AUGUSTA "			. 64
A VILLAGE LAY	. . .		. 66
A BRAND FROM THE BURNING			. 73
THE LOCUST-EATEN YEARS	.		. 79
HOW SHOULD I LIKE TO DIE ?			. 82
KING DAVID	. . .		. 84

vi *CONTENTS.*

SONNETS—*continued.*

	PAGE
CHRIST AT THE DOOR	89
COMPLETED JOY	93
THE SLEEP	95
GOD'S CHASTENINGS	97
THE SORROWFUL SEA	100
MISERERE, DOMINE!	102
THE CHALLENGE TO THE SWORD	104
THE CHALLENGE ANSWERED	106
FROM THE DUST	109
IN MEMORIAM, W. D. CREWDSON	111
WHAT IS YOUR LIFE?	113
EVER WITH GOD	116
ON THE DEATH OF THE REV. HENRY WRIGHT	118
A PROTEST	123

MISCELLANEOUS—

	PAGE
THE CONVENT GRATE	129
WILLIAM D'ALBINEY	144
A LEGEND OF THE LAKES	157
LINES FOR MUSIC	172

" I am no poet, and have never studied the laws of poetry ;
but I do desire devoutly to express those harmonious moods
of my spirit, with which God doth visit me, in harmonious
numbers."

EDWARD IRVING.

SONGS IN THE TWILIGHT.

▲

THE TWILIGHT.

THERE lieth a silence on all the house,
    A stillness as of the tomb:
Nothing is stirring—not even a mouse,
    In the wainscoting of the room.
       Nought is heard but the rain
       'Gainst the window-pane,
Like the sigh of a soul not cleansed from its stain.

Here as I sit by the light of the fire
    Far into the night alone,
Watching the flame as in many a spire
    It curls from the old hearth-stone,
       Plaintive thoughts come and go,
       Now they ebb, now they flow,
Borne in waves from the shore of the long-ago.

And many a face of the dead and dear
    Looks across from that distant shore,

And many a voice is heard in mine ear,
  Now silent for evermore.
          And I dream by the blaze,
          Of the far, sweet days,
Which pass in their glory before my gaze.

The fair golden times are with me again,
  When I roamed the fields a boy;
When I sang to the echoes that answered the strain,
  With notes of a mocking joy :
          Days of brightness they were,
          Not a cloud or a care,
A May-time with blossom and beauty fair.

The hedges once more with the thorn are white,
  And the breezes about me play;
The green meadow-grass with the dew is bright,
  And scents are blown from the hay :
          While the clear little stream,
          With a flash and a gleam,
Sounds sweet as some melody heard through a dream.

I wander again 'neath the beechen shade,
  Where the sunbeams glint and glide,

Out to the pleasant and open glade
  With daisies and buttercups pied :
      And the blue pigeons coo,
      As they used to do,
While a mate for their nest they tenderly woo.

And as loved ones return with the olden charms
  From the silent and ghostly land,
I reach forth my longing and empty arms,
  To the places whereon they stand :
      For they come in the light,
      Of the embers bright,
And together we talk in low tones through the night.

Thus I muse and I dream by the fire alone,
  Through the shadows to morning grey ;
And I feel that the bloom from my life has gone,
  And its colour is lost to the day :
      Anon, I grow calm,
      Hope sheddeth her balm,
And God in the night gives a song and a psalm.

Though the present be dark, I know that the dawn
  Will break, with its beauty and bloom,

That soon I shall hear from the dewy lawn
  The songs of birds in my room :
      And my heart will sing too,
      With a music as true,
As when smiles were many and tears were few.

I think :—God is Love : He takes, but He lives
  To repair the great grief He hath sent ;
As in nature, His hand ever tenderly gives
  The green lichen to cover the rent :
      Spring cometh again,
      With its sun and its rain,
And summer brings flowers to gladden the plain.

LOVE'S QUESTIONINGS.

WHEN dead they carry me beyond the door,
   And you sit lonely in our pleasant room,
  Will thoughts of days that can return no more,
    Rise up like ghosts that come back from the tomb?

Will tendernesses of the olden time,
  That lent a sweetness to the vanished hours,
Which, as they passed, struck each with silver chime,
  Be borne to you like scent of withered flowers?

O Love! will you remember that dear hour,
  The day when first I called you all my own,
When blossomed all my heart in sudden flower,
  And hope full-statured at a bound had grown?

Then spring was in its fresh and April grace,
  Its odours borne to us in breezes soft;
Beauty and bloom were brightening every place,
  The little lambs were bleating in the croft.

That spring !   Its sweetness comes across me now,
   I see the dewy fields that round us lay,
I feel its coolness on my fevered brow ;
   Ah, earth was nearer heaven that happy day !

Do you remember it ? and will it be
   A thought to comfort you when I am gone,
When I myself am but a memory,
   And you sit musing at our hearth alone ?

And what of after years when life grew sweet,
   When love robbed grief of more than half its pain,
And days passed rapidly on flying feet,—
   Will there be yearnings they could come again ?

Oh, will you sicken for the dear dead days,
   So happy, though they *had* some grief and care ?
And will your glass reflect a weary face,
   Pale with the passion of a sad despair ?

For those were days, beloved, when e'en our sighs
   Were often born of happiness, not pain ;
And life was like the blue and summer skies,
   Where, if a cloud appeared, it passed again.

So, will your heart ache as you sit and dream
   Fondly of me, now in the silent land,
Whence looking wistfully across the stream,
   I long to welcome you to where I stand ?

If able, I will come unto the place
   Where I sat with you, in the days gone by ;
And, as I look unseen into your face,
   You'll feel, by love's true instinct, I am nigh.

So do not weep, beloved, when I am gone ;
   Why should there fall for me one fruitless tear ?
In life, or death, you still are all my own ;
   What matter, then, if I be there or here ?

EFFIE.

"Love knows the secret of grief."
—MRS. BARRETT BROWNING.

SHE was here a little child,
  Not so very long ago;
Then spring-airs were blowing mild,
  Now the earth is cold with snow.
Then she was so young and bright,
Flashing like a gleam of light,
Playing 'midst the daisies white.

Out and in amongst the trees,
  'Neath the shadows cool and green;
Buoyant as the summer breeze
  Which the branches played between.
How she floated here and there,
Spirit-like, and sweet and fair,
Scarce of earth and more of air!

Often have I seen her pass
  Through the young and sprouting corn,
Stealing gently through the grass,
  Looking if the larks were born.
Or a butterfly she'd chase,
With a flush upon her face,
And a nameless winsome grace.

Lovely grew she day by day—
  Hair of gold and eyes of blue;
Fresh as any flower in May;
  Trusting, innocent, and true.
Lips as red as rosy wine,
Looks, although so infantine,
Seeing into things divine.

Music made she in our home;
  Light she brought with her, and joy;
Hearts leaped up to see her come,
  Now so bashful, now so coy.
Ah, she was the sweetest thing!
Soft her voice, with silvery ring,
Like as when a bird doth sing.

Dead ;—for me she liveth still,
　Goeth with me where I go ;
Tears for her run down at will,
　All my heart they overflow.
For my darling she is gone,
And I stand here all alone,
Looking at her grave-yard stone.

Oh, my Effie, dearest dear !
　On this tomb I see thy name,
Graven there well-nigh a year,
　Since God's angels for thee came.
Oh, my own, my little one,
Thou thy race hast quickly run—
Ended it, ere well begun !

Does that twelvemonth seem to thee
　Short, my darling ; not a year ?
Very long it seems to me,
　Not an hour without its tear.
Short to thee ;—for at thy feet
God has placèd all things sweet ;
Heavenly joys, for heaven meet.

Thou art where the angels move,
　Up and down before God's face,
And where He whose name is Love,
　Doth all things in love embrace.
Thou hast, Effie, entered in
That safe place where is no sin ;
Far from earth, and earth's sad din.

In thine hand a harp of gold,
　Struck beneath the green life-tree,
Maketh music manifold ;
　Ah, that it could reach to me !
Smiles are ever in thine eyes ;
Smiles as if for victories,
Won o'er Heaven's mysteries.

Dost thou ever downward look
　On the world, so poor and vain ?
Hast for ever from thee shook
　Thoughts of all its care and pain ?
Is to thee the past *quite* past,
Nothing better than a waste,
All its memories effaced ?

And thy father, Effie, say
　　Has he grown a something dim?
Hast with earth put far away
　　Thoughts and memories of him?
Dost thou never, darling, miss,
Just as I do, all the bliss
When our mouths met kiss to kiss?

I would know if thou dost hear
　　Voices that I send to thee;
Do they trouble the calm sphere,
　　Discords in its melody?
Dost thou, sweet one, ever long
I the angels were among,
Joining in their choral song?

Lost, beloved, but lovèd still;
　　Do the thoughts of days behind
Ever through thy spirit thrill,
　　Press themselves upon thy mind?
And do wishes rise in vain
Days gone by might come again,
That the *now* were as the *then?*

Effie, 'midst the children there
   I shall know thee; claim thee mine:
Hardly, dear one, grown more fair,
   Though transfigured to divine.
I shall know thee from the rest,
Hold thee ever to this breast,
Of all bliss and thee possest.

Ah, I wrong myself and thee,
   Fretting thus against the rod!
Thou art happy:—let it be:
   Rest, until I come, with God.
And I know that soon the door,
Opening on the other shore,
Will receive me evermore.

ONE LOOK.

NE look, but only one,
Within the veil where God doth show His face;
Once but to see the radiance of the Throne;
But once, the wonders of that glorious place;
One look, but only one,
Should I not wish the weary race were run?

Could I but hear one song,
Sung by the angels in harmonious voice,
Floating the heart of heaven all along,
As evermore they worship and rejoice;
Could I but hear one song,
To join that glorious choir should I not long?

Could I the loved enfold,
Taking the lost within these arms once more,
To press them to my yearning heart, and hold,
As I have done in happy days of yore;

Could I the loved enfold,
To front grim Death should I not then be bold?

Then should I, day by day,
Before the golden doors of heaven wait;
Watching for this alone, and this alway,
That God would ope for me the blessèd gate;
Then should I, day by day,
Long like a prisoned bird to flee away.

B

MAY.

THE day is clear, the air is cool,
    The streamlet runs with murmurs sweet ;
The swallows skim along the pool,
    The lark is singing o'er the wheat.

The spring is in its early pride,
    Dressing each branch and spray with green ;
And flowers bloom on every side,
    In hedge-rows and in thickets seen.

Across the corn the west winds blow,
    In beechen woods doves coo and pair ;
The cattle in the pastures low,
    The cuckoo's voice is everywhere.

'Tis joy to breathe on such a day,
    When beauty spreads before the eyes,
To catch the fragrance of the May,
    To see the splendour of the skies.

The spring it maketh all things new,
    The fields, the trees ; the very sod,
While sparkling with the morning dew,
    Seems fresh as from the hand of God.

Let us be glad in these sweet hours,
    In all God giveth us to-day :
The birds, the leaves, the op'ning flowers,
    For soon must glide from us the May.

I would not that a care should cast
    A shadow over heart or brow,
What though the spring will soon be past ?
    I'd live within the happy now.

The thought of Autumn with its chill,
    Of Winter with its snows and frosts,
Need not our sky with shadows fill,
    Our hearts with sense of pleasures lost.

God gives us now this world so fair,
    Why think we what far morrows bring?
Does He not clothe the lily fair?
    Feed careless sparrow on the wing?

Each fragile blossom on its stem,
   Each bird that carols in the air,
Leaves God on high to think for them,
   And knows not either want or care,

They teach us well to trust His love,
   Our hearts with happy faith to fill,
To learn from all beneath, above,
   " Sufficient to the day the ill."

A SOLDIER'S STORY.

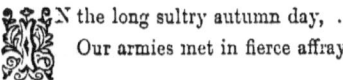N the long sultry autumn day, .
　　Our armies met in fierce affray

England and France were then at war,
Fighting in Spanish fields afar.

The corn that ripened on the plain
Was red with blood of brave men slain ;

And, trampled 'neath the horses' tread,
Formed a last pillow for the dead.

All day our ranks stood firm and fast,
Though thinned by many a rifle-blast ;

Our men fought bravely, bravely fell,
Mowed down by iron shot and shell.

At last, before the stronger force
Retired we all, both foot and horse,

Hoping in our retreat to gain
A river swoll'n with summer's rain—

Meaning to place its broad, deep flow,
Between us and th' advancing foe.

Our troops plunged in the rapid flood,
Swam through, and on the far bank stood ;

Then, pressing to the higher ground,
Rank after rank in order wound

Up the steep height ; no hint of dread
Was heard in their fierce tramp and tread.

We sought to gain the wooded hill,
Marching to trump and bugle shrill ;

But paused just half way up to see
How with the foemen it might be—

And wishing, too, to give one cheer
To fret and taunt the Frenchman's ear.

On turning round, there met our sight,
Where swarmed the foe to left and right,

And where our tents had lately stood,
Beyond the rushing torrent's flood,

A woman! A great shudder ran
Through all our troops from rear to van.

This woman was a soldier's wife,
A man sore hurt in that day's strife.

We bore him with us faint and stunned,
And bleeding from a gun-shot wound.

Poor thing! she had been left behind,
Passed by, o'erlooked, or out of mind.

Trembling she stood, wild with alarm,
With face all pale, and outstretched arm,

In dumb appeal. Her frenzied cry
Lost in the roar of the stream hard by.

"Halt!" As they hear that stern command,
Silently turn our men, and stand.

"What man will go, on foot or horse,
And save a life from death,—or worse?"

Our Captain sprang from out the rank,
Struck spurs into his horse's flank—

The snorting steed, in mettled might,
Started, and dashed right down the height.

We saw them then in the current's tide,
Cleaving the waves to the other side.

Rifle and rifle sent forth its ball,
Bullets like raindrops round them fall,

And the waters hiss, and flash, and steam,
Under the shot that ruffles the stream.

Our Captain, caring not, rode on,
Till at length the farther side was won.

He reached the shore without a wound,
And climbed the bank near the Frenchman's ground,

Then pricked his horse, and gained the place
Where the woman stood with awe-struck face—

And terror in her straining eye,
Lest he had only come to die.

He bent an instant; stooping low,
He swung her up to his saddle-bow;

He turned in haste his horse's head,
And plunged again in the river's bed.

Our hearts beat fast as we saw him come;
We hardly breathed; stood still, and dumb;

But he rode not now a ride of death,
There was no need to hold our breath!

The French had dropped their muskets all;
No bullets whiz, no ring of ball,

Came whirring on our Captain's ear—
No cause he had for care or fear;

For the cheer from the British lines that rose
Was echoed back by our gallant foes,

Whose hearts were stirred by that brave deed,
When our Captain bore, on panting steed,

Back to our camp the soldier's wife,
Rescued at risk of limb and life.

WAR TIME.

SILENTLY they sat together—not a whisper, not
    a word;
    Only now and then a sobbing or a shuddering
    sigh was heard.
Two sad women weeping sorely,—Robert's mother and
    his bride;
One was bent with years and sorrow, one was in her
    youthful pride.
Yet both hearts were torn with anguish; life for them
    had lost its bloom,
Grief made wreck of all the future, not a ray to pierce
    the gloom.

War, with all its bloody horrors, broke out many months
    ago,
And there came the urgent summons, calling men to meet
    the foe;

There was gath'ring of the regiments, sounds of muster
    far and near,
Neigh of horses, martial music, trumpet-blast, and clarion
    clear.
When the country asked for soldiers, who would dare to
    shrink from fight?
All would strike for hearth and altar: for the true and
    for the right.

All alive the Minster City with the call of bugle-horn,
With the clash and clink of armour, and the muster night
    and morn;
Horses champed in street and stable, neighed as if they
    smelt afar,
Borne for leagues across the valley, scent of strife and
    coming war.
Every place was filled with clamour, noise of jingling spur
    and sword,
And, through all, the ring of rifle and the roll of drums
    were heard.

Robert marched with other soldiers,—parted from his
    clinging wife:
Three months only were they wedded, ere there came the
    sound of strife;

And she bore herself right bravely, blessed him as she saw
    him go,
For she felt he was his country's, and had noble work to
    do !
But when came the last embraces, when she said the long
    " Good-bye,"
Then she felt the pang of parting, was as pang of those
    who die.

They had loved from early childhood,—loved each other
    girl and boy,
Played together in the meadows, shared each other's grief
    and joy ;
Plucked the sweet and fragrant flowers in the long, bright
    summer days,
Wandered all along the river, or through tangled wood-
    land ways,
Knelt together in the Minster, where their prayers went
    up to heaven,
In the flush of early morning, or the hush of solemn even.

He had never told his feelings,—she had never probed her
    own,
Till one evening in the May-time as they watched the sun
    go down,

Flushing all the hills with colour, making all the land-
    scape bright,
To his heart came sudden rapture, filling all his eye with
    light ;
And he poured out his deep passion,—breathed it in a
    willing ear,
Told her how he loved her truly, and had loved for many
    a year.

As he spake she blushed and trembled, thrilled to hear
    his fervent tale,
Vainly tried to find an answer, voice and words both
    seemed to fail.
But at length there came a whisper in a low and under-
    tone,—
She was his, and ever had been—ever would be his alone.
Life would not be life without him—of that life he was
    a part ;
Yes ! she loved him dearly : only : with her woman's
    tender heart !

All the orchards were in blossom,—bloom on every
    branch and bough,
Bloom on pear, and peach, and apple, like great heaps of
    scented snow ;

All the copses rang with singing, and the lark sang in the
    blue,
And the world was filled with music, and their hearts
    were singing too.
All about them was so dream-like,—all so new, so very
    sweet.
Hardly knew they if the heavens were above or 'neath
    their feet.

They were one in vow and promise, as they were in heart
    before,
And that summer caught a beauty that till now no sum-
    mer wore ;
And the golden moon above them more than seemèd fair,
As to shining stars and planets she laid all her beauty
    bare ;
While the flowers that sprang around them, simplest
    daisy on the sod,
Like the bush that burnt for Moses, burned to them as
    if with God.

They were wedded in the Minster, where they often knelt
    to pray ;
Left it in a happy dream-land, not a shadow on their
    way.

Followed soon the sweet home-coming, with its rest, and
    peace, and grace ;
Love, with all its light and lustre, glorified the common-
    place.
And as days and weeks passed onward, each to other grew
    so dear,
That a new and happy Eden seemed to bless this nether
    sphere.

But their bliss was rudely broken : War came, filling
    homes with dread,
And with sad forecasting bodings of the wounded and
    the dead,
With farewells and bitter partings, last embraces, passion-
    ate cries,
Tears that started all unbidden from the heart to weep-
    ing eyes.
"Wife," in faltering tones said Robert—"I must go, and
    you must stay ;
Blessings on your head, my darling; think of me, dear
    love, and pray."

Mary and his aged mother lived together in one home,
Sought to comfort each the other till he back again should
    come ;

Bore with patience Robert's absence, went about their
    household ways,
Longed and hoped for his returning—passed as best they
    might their days;
Trembled when news came of battle, borne in rumour
    from afar;
Sickened as they heard of fighting, and the horrors of the
    war.

One sad morning brought the tidings, flashing all along
    the wire,
Of a long and bloody battle, where beneath a deadly fire
Hundreds were mowed down together in thick swathes
    along the plain,
But as yet no names were given—who were living, who
    were slain;
One thing only known as certain : All had nobly borne
    their part,
England well might bear their memory 'mongst the bravest
    on her heart.

Where was he—the son, the husband? Lying covered
    o'er with scars?
Sorely wounded? dead or dying, with his wan face to the
    stars?

Was he living, weak and helpless,—not a friend or kins-
man near?

Did he call for wife or mother? call for help, and they not hear?

Oh, where was he?   Christ in heaven! has the pity left
Thine eyes?

Has Thine ear grown dull and heavy?   Is it deaf to all
our cries?

Thus they spake while tears fell thickly, waiting till fresh
tidings came,

Dreading lest the next despatches should contain the husband's name.

Scanned they every list with terror, with a quiv'ring,
shrinking eye,

With a blind and sick'ning anguish, and a feeling they
must die,

If the fear that thrilled and shook them, should at once
take actual form,

And the muttering of the tempest burst upon them in the
storm.

Came at length the worst they dreaded.   In the list was
Robert's name,

'Mongst the men who sold life dearly, and it burnt them
like a flame:

c

Plain it lay upon the paper, just as if none else were
  there,—
And they turned upon each other one blank look of great
  despair;
Love and hope for them were over! earth was empty, life
  was vain !
In that moment nature taught them her capacities of pain.

Then a shriek, a cry of anguish, followed by a shuddering
  wail,
And they both sat broken-hearted,—sat with faces wild
  and pale;
Moved not, stirred not, sorrow-stricken,—just like statues,
  turned to stone,
Life and feeling lost in anguish: for the moment dead
  and gone—
Dry the eye-balls, seared and burning, not one tear did
  overflow;
Better stormy gusts of weeping, than this sullen, silent
  woe.

Mary rose at last quite calmly, to her heart his mother
  pressed,
Wound her loving arms around her, laid her head upon
  her breast,

Wailed forth sadly, "Mother! Mother!" gave a cry of
    sharpest pain;
Then the pent-up grief was loosened, came the tears like
    showers of rain,
And the women wept together, knelt, and prayed aloud
    to God;
Prayed for patience, sought for mercy, bent to kiss the
    chastening rod.

Followed days of desolation,—passing each with leaden
    pace,
Dark and gloomy was the present, and the future hard to face:
All the streams of life were frozen—gone its sweet and
    pleasant spring—
Love and joy, that once made sunshine, had for ever taken
    wing;
Hope had burned down to the socket; in its ashes lived
    no fire;
One great, dismal, helpless sorrow, slew the present, killed
    desire.

As they sat one summer's evening in the garden 'neath
    the shade,
Looking on the shining glory which the west'ring sunshine
    made,

Listening to the merry singing of the throstle in the tree,
Catching just the drowsy murmur in the linden of the
    bee,
Talking sometimes, sometimes silent, all their thoughts
    on that dear time
When he, too, was sitting with them, underneath this
    very lime—

Heard they through a pause a footstep, passing by the
    wicker gate ;
All they thought was,—" 'Tis some neighbour come to pay
    a visit late."
So they moved not at his coming, waiting till he reached
    the place,
Hoping then to bid him welcome, with the sad smile on
    their face.
Friends came oft to cheer the sorrow of their dark and
    lonely life,
Grieving for the mourning mother, for the early widowed
    wife !

As the steps drew nearer, closer, turned they round their
    heads to see—
God of grace !   Who stood before them ?   Some pale
    ghost ? or was it he ?

Throbbed their hearts, and thrilled their pulses, and their
   soul was in their eyes:
Ah, did graves give back their tenants? Did the dead
   from death arise?
Were they mad, or were they dreaming? Was he come
   to them once more?
Come to home, and arms all empty,—come to heal the
   hearts so sore?

Had suspense a moment longer held them in its cruel
   sway,
Mary must have maddened surely—brain and sense had
   given way.
There she stood with eyes dilated, brow and bosom all
   aflame,
While through parted lips the breathing in great shud-
   d'ring spasms came;
Then a cry—half shriek, half whisper—"Robert! Robert!
   is it you?
O my God, can this be real? Am I mad? Or is it true?"

"Mary! Mother! Darling Mary!" And the voice upon
   her ear
Sounded like a voice from heaven,—banished every doubt
   and fear.

Then she sprang into his arms, dropped her face upon his
    breast,
Wept sweet tears of holy rapture, with a sense of blessèd
    rest ;
Felt this hour was compensation for the anguish now
    gone by,
Felt if death had come that moment, then it were most
    blest to die.

Fondly gazed they on their lost one—found again—their
    own—their own—
Who brought back to life its sweetness when all hope was
    dead and gone :
Saw that he was bronzed and bearded, and on either
    cheek a scar,
Thought he never looked so noble, as with those deep
    marks of war ;
For they spake of dauntless courage, how he braved the
    shot and shell,
Bore him in the battle bravely, rushed through fire and
    smoke of hell.

Then he told them all his story, how he had been left for
    slain,
'Mongst a heap of dead and dying, on the bloody battle-plain;

How they found him faint and bleeding, with a wound on
    breast and head ;

How for weeks he was unconscious, lying on a fever-bed ;

How life conquered in the struggle, after long delirious
    days ;

"Nay, what matter now, my darling ? to our God be all
    the praise."

THE SUMMERS OF THE LONG AGO.

"I sleep, but my heart waketh."

HEN silence falls upon the solemn night,
    And all in house and street is hushed and
        still,
Bright visions rise before my happy sight,
    And come and go at will;
        And days long fled,
Ghosts of the past, come to me from the dead.

And friends I see in dreams, as fair and sweet
    As were the summers of the long ago,
When in the golden days we used to meet
    And talk in voices low,
        And often stand
Within the sphere of an enchanted land.

Awake, I die; in dreams, I live again,
    For then return the hopes I knew of old;
Ere I had wept, or love had grown to pain,
        And left me sad and cold;
            When all the hours
Were scented with the fragrant breath of flowers.

So when the waking comes, it comes too soon,
    For with it pass my bright and blessèd dreams;
My sun sinks suddenly; goes down at noon;
        Leaving behind no gleams;
            Gone is my spring,
And life becomes a wintry frozen thing.

So would I dream, and wake, and dream again—
    O love! O hope! come back a little while.
What though the wak'ning must be full of pain?
        In blissful sleep I smile—
            Come vanished years,
Let me dream still, although I wake to tears!

LIFE'S CONTRASTS.

E wooed her in the sweet spring days,
  When flowers were scenting all the air,
And soft winds whispered in the leaves,
  And skies were blue, and life was fair.

He won her on a summer eve,
  Beneath a stretch of purple sky,
And through the fields they walked that night,
  Pledged to each other till they die.

Upon them fell the sweet moonshine:
  Was it a dream? or was it true?
The world at once had grown so bright
  That sooth to say they hardly knew.

He wedded her in the long, long days;
  The bells rang out; he bore her home;
And time flew by on rapid wing—
  Across two lives new light had come.

Dear household ways, and household truth,
  And homely peace, and gentle cheer ;
And days and nights of full content,
  In which each grew to each more dear.

Then came a boy to crown their love,
  With rose-bud lips for mother's kiss,
To give the earth a richer joy,
  To lend each day a fresher bliss.

Ah ! why should summers ever wane,
  Or tempest sweep across the sky ;
Or change pass o'er a happy dream—
  Love grow to pain ;—and pleasures die ?

Why should the face be wan with grief,
  Or heart, o'ercharged with weight of care,
Sicken beneath a hope deferred,
  And nurse a keen and dark despair ?

Why not all life be as that night,
  'Mid breath of flowers—'neath shining skies,
When the fair girl was wooed as wife,
  With whispered words and sweet replies ?

The din of war shook all the land,
   And harshly grated on the ear,
And loving homes sent forth their best,
   And loving hearts forced back the tear.

The cause of freedom, truth, and right,
   Summoned the noble and the brave;
And he must march down to the West,
   And fill, if need, a soldier's grave.

"He dared not shrink from such a call,"
   So spoke he to the trembling wife;
Where others went he too must go,
   Honour was dearer far than life!

She listened weeping to his words,
   Close held him to her breaking heart,
And all the world grew dark and cold;
   'Twas death in life from him to part.

" Dora, my wife, my life, my love,
   The great God lives in yonder sky;
Trust Him ;—I leave but for a time :
   Is He not, darling, always nigh?

"Sweet heart, lift up thy drooping head;
   Look with brave eyes straight into mine;
When far away on tented field,
   Their light will often on me shine.

"I would be strong, not weak, true wife—
   Help me to say the last 'good-bye;'
For here, or there, where'er I be,
   Am I not thine until I die?

"Yea, after death: if I should fall
   'Mid battle's storm upon the plain,
Thou and our boy will join me soon;
   And life is little: death is gain."

Then, after many a clinging kiss,
   He gently tore himself away;
And she, with sorrow in her heart,
   Was left alone to wait and pray.

She sought for patience, and was calm—
   She stilled the sorrow at her heart;
She went about her household ways—
   The child to soothe her did his part.

So went the days, a weary round,
  Telling each other as they passed,
All bearing this one weight of care—
  And still the saddest was the last.

Then flashed a message 'neath the sea,
  Which smote upon the startled ear,
And emptied Christmas homes of joy,
  Filling a nation's heart with fear.

A battle had been fought and won,
  The balls of death left many slain,
Hundreds died fighting in the breach,
  Hundreds lay wounded on the plain.

A whole brigade was under fire,
  Each shot a gallant soldier's knell;
Hardly a man escaped with life,
  So murd'rous was the fatal shell—

Friends came to break the fatal news,
  But faltered, and their voices shook;
She raised her eyes in sudden fear,
  And searched each face with eager look—

And when she heard that he had died
   Amongst the foremost in the fight,
The hand of death was at her heart,
   And on her fell a cloud like night.

They strove to speak some healing words,
   To take from sorrow's edge the pain—
Poor breaking heart ! What comfort now ?—
   With love both life and hope were slain.

Then with a brain all sick and blind,
   And with a sharp, unconscious cry,
Stricken, she shrank upon the ground :
   Ah, well indeed if she could die !

But not for her such sweet release ;
   She woke to life, not love again ;
And crept about as one whose heart
   Is daily hurt by some great pain.

She bowed her head to God's decree,
   "Thy will," she meekly said, " be done ; "
But the deep wound still bled within,
   And often forced from her a moan.

Her child too sickened, pined, and died ;
  And when she laid it in its shroud,
She wept, but not as mothers weep,
  Whose grief is violent and loud.

She could not sorrow for the boy,
  That she had given life to save,
But only wished she too could die,
  And lie beside him in the grave.—

Her face grew hollow, and a fire
  Like crimson burned on either cheek ;
Her eyes had caught the wistful look
  Of one who far-off worlds doth seek.

They buried her in winter days,
  When all the land was white with snow ;
Thankful to God her pain had passed,
  And restful death had crowned her woe.

SONNETS.

D

REFLECTIONS.

I.

 STOOD beside a sheltered tranquil lake,
　　When earth wore all the holy hush and calm
　　That in a temple follow prayer and psalm.
Nature kept Sabbath : not a breath did shake
A leaf, or branch, or dew-drop in the brake,
And winds were still, and every air was balm ;
And as I gazed into the waters sweet,
All heaven seemed lying at my very feet.
Far in the depths, translucent, pure and clear,
Unruffled even by a ripple's flow,
Were glassed the stars that in the azure sphere
With silver fires made all the skies aglow.
And yearned I then that, as within that mere,
High heaven were mirror'd in my heart below.

II.

I would that heaven *were* mirror'd in my heart,
Distinct, defined, as in this tranquil lake,
Which each reflection is so quick to take
That here it sleeps, the sky's true counterpart,
With not a cloudlet passing it athwart.
See, in its depths a thousand glories shine,
Flooded and fulgent with a light divine.
Ah, would that I were only as thou art,
Thou mirror, radiant with celestial sheen !
Thou glass, to image forth that world on high
Which o'er me in its tender grace doth lean,
Clad in a fair and stainless purity !
O God, that heaven in me were clearly seen,
As yonder stars within this wave serene!

THE LAKE COUNTRY.

I.

LAND of wondrous beauty, where each scene
   Reveals fresh grandeur and some novel grace ;
   Where glory clothes from sunny top to base
The hills which spring from lakes and meadows green ;
Where tarns, blue as the skies which o'er them lean,
Lie cradled in the mountains' fond embrace,
That bend to see themselves within their face.
Lovely at all times ; either when the rain
Comes driving 'thwart the heavens from rifted cloud ;
Or shrieks the storm like some lost soul in pain ;
Or roaring thunder wakes the echoes loud.
Most beautiful when valleys smile again,
And landscapes throwing off their misty shroud,
The golden sunlight glorifies the plain.

II.

No spot without its beauty, far or near ;
Green glen and glade, huge scaur, and wood-clothed hill,
Fair field and fell, and silver mountain-rill,
And lakes where lilies, flowering all the mere,
Glass their white loveliness in waters clear
That sleep beneath them, pure and cool and still.
Here have I drunk of beauty to my fill.
As friends who better known become more dear,
So with thy charms.   When life draws near the end,
Ye shall be with me, hills and valleys green ;
And dying eyes from dying bed shall send
A yearning look to each remembered scene,
Fresh in my heart as though beheld yestreen ;
And thoughts of you with hopes of heaven shall blend.

PAST AND PRESENT.

I.

OLD scenes are here ; here is the ivied grange,
  And here the lake, the valley, and the hill,
  The wood, the stream that turns the busy mill—
The same as when by them I used to range.
Though years have fled, yet nothing looketh strange,
And as I gaze the Past seems with me still ;
The Past ! the thought of which has power to thrill—
The same, yet not the same.   There is a change,
And all around a different aspect wears.
What is it ?   Friends, the good and true, are gone,
And with them gone the charm of happy years,
And much that hope had fondly built upon ;
So from my heart well up unbidden tears,
For dear ones who have left me one by one.

II.

Ah me ! I sicken for the dear old days,
When friends and youth and joy enriched the time,
And all came well : summer, or winter's rime,
December's cold, or sweet and blooming Mays,
The stretch of wold, or shady forest-ways,
Scent of bright gorse, or wafts of fragrant thyme,
Silence of noon, or birds' song in the Lime ;
And yet I feel the old charm as I gaze—
'Tis gone ! departed with the friends, who lie
Nearer than all to hearts that yearn in vain,
To keep them still,—not keeping them to die :—
'Twas they who made the light of days gone by.
Our crown of sorrow this,—its keenest pain,—
Loved ones must go, and only *things* remain.

III.

Yet be it so.   Glide on, thou rushing stream ;
Raise still your tops to heaven, ye sunlit hills ;
Flash down the mountain's side, ye foaming rills ;
And wear, ye valleys, still your radiant gleam,
The tender beauty of the Painter's dream.

If friends must go, they only seem to die ;
Lost for a time to touch and ear and eye ;
And passed a moment from our loving sight,
But yet to be restored to our embrace.
For if like them we seek the true and right,
Clad in the strength of love's transcendent grace,
And climb the upward path from height to height,
We too shall stand where God's uplifted face
Fills all high heaven's sphere with holy light.

NIAGARA.*

I.

ET there be silence; it befits a scene
  Glorious as when God first pronounced all good;
  Let not the world upon the thoughts intrude,
For He is here who through all time hath been.
His greatness in the cataract is seen,
Whose rush of whirling waters offers food
For solemn meditation's reverent mood.
Oh, let the eye be vigilant, and keen
To hold the torrent leaping from yon height,
Pure, radiant, glittering, exquisitely clear,
Till worlds of beauty open on the sight,
And earth and all its trifles disappear.
So to thine ear the loud harmonious roar
Will come with echoes from the eternal shore.

* September 1879.

II.

How fine the sweep of seething billowy sea,
Which o'er the precipice so grandly breaks,
And with its thunders earth and heaven shakes,
As down it rolls in awful majesty,
Untamed, unfettered, strong, resistless, free,
Fed by the waters of four mighty lakes !
The foaming cataract, a joy to see,
The awed and dazzled eye with beauty takes,
As o'er the rock green sheets of emerald flow,
Which rise again in clouds of luminous spray,
While the sun smites the mists till rainbows glow
To crown the waters, which upon their way
Impetuous hurry to the gulf below,
In milk-white torrents of tumultuous snow.

THE HORSE-SHOE FALLS.

III.

HAFED seas of weltering waters met in fight,
Confusèd floods, mingled in wild affray,
Plunge crashing downwards in their headlong
    might,
And in the wild abyss are churned to spray,
Then tossed to heaven in tremulous clouds of white,
Making a glory of the common day.
Beyond imagination is this sight,
This rush of waters roaring on their way.
Here, as I stand, watching the torrent's leap,
There comes across the current, borne to me,
Voices as from a far eternity,
Music of many waters loud and deep,
Scene beyond words ! glories of fall and stream,
Ye wake a transport and a joy supreme.

IV.

If ye are glorious ye are awful too,
And touch the springs of terror at their source,
As watch we your inexorable force,
And feel your pity it were vain to woo.
For, deaf to voice of prayer, ye would pursue
All pitiless and passionless your course ;
Nothing your flashing waters would subdue,
With all the thunders of the ages hoarse.
We quail before you, torrents, in your pride ;
The strongest swimmer caught within your power
Were but your plaything, helpless as the flower
Borne on the rapids' swift resistless tide.
Ah, well that o'er the chasm deep and broad
The rainbow glitters like the smile of God !

LIFE.

LIFE, Life, Life ! O full and bounteous Life !
   Bright with thy glowing suns and mellow moons,
   And homes with smiles and happy faces rife ;
Fair morns, and tender eves, and amber noons,—
I love thee and this upper world, the flowers,
The woods, the dells, the streams, and grassy glade,
The quiet forest-paths where leafy bowers
By interlacing boughs are greenly made.
Well love I too the joyous birds' sweet song,
That fills the copses in the budding spring ;
Yet for a higher life than this I long,
Which will with it a true completeness bring ;
And did the Dove's swift power to me belong,
I'd prune for upward flight my rapid wing.

DEATH.

DEATH, Death, Death! unlovely, cruel Death!
Grim King of Terrors, with thy barbèd dart!
Why should I fear thee, dreadful though thou art,
Or speak thy name with low and bated breath,
And eyes that fill with swelling tears beneath
Their quivering lids, as throbs my timid heart?
Why should I shrink at thought of thee, or start?
What though thy curse still sadly lingereth?
Nought art thou but the travail pangs before
The birth which ushers in a higher life;
The surge which bears the vessel to that shore
Where storms shall rage no more, and joys are rife;
A Port of quiet rest for evermore,
Beyond the reach of sorrow, sin, and strife.

"PER ANGUSTA AD AUGUSTA."

THIS INSCRIPTION IS PLACED OVER THE DOOR OF AN OLD
HOUSE IN COIRE.

I.

" THROUGH narrow things to great." So the
words run,
Carved in rude letters 'bove an antique door ;
And as I scanned the legend o'er and o'er,
Busy imagination had begun
To muse what truth could from the scroll be won.
This first : Oft through the dark and grim defile,
We reach the open where rich cornfields smile,
And grapes grow purple 'neath the mellow sun.
Thus, oft through Duty's uninviting gate
We enter on a broad and rich domain,

And win the triumphs that on virtue wait,
Reaching through seeming loss the highest gain.
All pass this straitened door who would be great ;
And find in front an ever-widening plain.

II.

" From narrow things to great."   The words might stand
Fit motto for Death's portal, grim and black,
From which we shrink and shudder, and look back
With yearning eyes on this familiar land
Where we have lived and loved, enjoyed and planned.
But think we that upon the other side
This gate is life ; beyond, it opens wide
On everlasting hills, aglow with light,
Caught from the lustrous shinings of God's face,
Scenes of surpassing beauty and delight,
Rivers of pleasure, noons without a night,
Marvels of glory and surpassing grace ?
Ah, fools and blind, to tremble at the door
Through which we pass to joys for evermore.

A VILLAGE LAY.

IXTEEN to-day, just sweet sixteen,
   She moves along with step of queen,
   The sunshine clasps in warm embrace
Her youthful form, and radiant face.
Pure her cheek, as the snow-wreath fair,
Like ruddy gold her curling hair.
     Then ring, oh bells, oh strong and clear,
     Chime out your music on the ear ;
     Sweetly, oh sweetly let it flow,
     From your turret tower to men below.

See ! she comes up the garden way,
Fresh as the dawn of an April day,
Clad in a kirtle green, like spring,
She with her scent of flowers doth bring.
Her child-eyes, full of sweet content,
Look on the world in wonderment.

O ring out, bells ! oh clear and strong,
And as ye swing the notes prolong :
Tell out, tell out, to all who hear,
The birthday 'tis of one so dear.

Glad parents of such maiden sweet !
Proud ground that feels the little feet !
Rich gems that glisten on her breast !
Oh happy rose, to her bosom prest !
She moves among the lilies tall,
Herself the fairest lily of all.
    Ring out, oh bells, oh loudly ring :
    Out on the breeze your rich strains fling,
    And swell until the silver sound
    Is wafted all the country round !

Two summers have flown quickly by,
The flowers bloom, the flowers die ;
Two winters clothe the earth with snows,
But lightly touch our sweetest rose.
They bear to her the crown of life,
Betrothèd maid—then happy wife.
    Ring out, oh bells ! ring out your chime,
    Glad tidings give of this golden time ;

Oh ring and swing from your turrets high,
And bless the ears of the passers-by !

She cometh up the alleys green,
With drooping head and modest mien ;
Her bridesmaids follow close behind,
'Neath veils just stirred by the whispering wind.
Now she has reached the carvèd porch,
And now has entered holy church.

Ring, ring, oh bells ! but soft and low,
And let your music sweetly flow ;
Floating along the charmèd air,
As suits the hour of holy prayer.

And now she kneels a happy bride,
The bridegroom kneeling at her side ;
And prayers ascend to God above,
For peace, and joy, and truth, and love ;
And o'er each bowed and reverent head
The prayer is made, the blessing said.

Ring out, ring out ! again, again !
Ring out, oh bells, a joyful strain !
Another peal, to swell and die
In notes of sweetest harmony !

Plighted the troth, the ring is given,
And one they are in sight of Heaven.
Slowly they leave the house of prayer,
Both so young, and one so fair;
And people bless them as they tread
By grassy graves of the sainted dead.
    Then ring, oh bells! oh, sweeter still;
    And as ye all the silence fill,
    Give promise rich of the coming time—
    Sound out, sound out, a full-voiced chime!

Their home is lighted from above
With trustful faith, and fervent love,
And happy hope, and deep content,
And pleasures sweet and innocent.
And children come—a girl and boy—
To fill their brimming cup with joy.
    Ring on, oh bells, ring as of yore!
    But still more joyful than before;
    Tell of bright hours and cloudless days,
    Of peace and prayer and grateful praise.

Oh happy time! oh pleasant years!
So full of smiles, so scant of tears!

Alas ! that life's full harmony
Should pass into the minor key,
And death turn passion into pain,
And prayer be fruitless, love be vain !
  Ring, then, ye chimes, but soft and low—
  Solemn and sad, toll out our woe.
  Oh ring a muffled, deep-toned knell,
  The mournful peal of passing bell !

Oh Angel with the purple wings !
That o'er all life a shadow flings ;
Death ! thou dost teach the heart to sound
The depths of agony profound.
When sorrow, voiceless as the tomb,
Weeps in the silence, and is dumb.
  Then ring, ye bells, a deep, sad knell,
  In solemn tones of last farewell ;
  Nor balm nor lethe for such ill,
  The gnawing grief will live on still.

Death claimed as his the tender wife ;
The husband's joy, life of his life :
He saw her drooping day by day,
As droops the flower and fades away,

Until at last she passed and fled,
And the living stood above the dead.
 Oh ring, ye bells, a muffled peal,
 Which on the ear shall slowly steal;
 Sadly swing again, again,
 As well befits a day of pain.

A long procession, winding slow,
Doth through the churchyard darkly go;
Mourners and bearers weeping all,
As with trembling hands they bear the pall—
And now they pause,—the words are said
Which tell of rest for the sainted dead.
 Oh bells! toll solemnly, oh, toll!
 From the world has passed a loving soul.
 Dead is she, the tender wife,—
 Dead in the bloom and bliss of life.

Toll! "Earth to earth, and dust to dust."
Toll! sobs are drowned in words of trust.
Toll! tears flow fast as, still and cold,
They lay her down in the churchyard mould.
Toll, toll again, oh sad bells, toll!
On the troubled ear your dirges roll.

Yet hope doth mingle with your sound,
And light breaks through grief's night profound.
For " Blest the dead,"—so says " the Word,"—
" Who dying rest in Christ the Lord."

A BRAND FROM THE BURNING.

T was a close and stifling summer day,
    The August sun blazed hot upon the street ;
The little children were too tired to play,
    And on the pavement was no sound of feet.

I passed through many an alley, many a lane,
    Until I reached a low half-opened door,
Whose panels bore the mark of blotch and stain,
    And with foul words were smirched and scribbled o'er.

This was the house I sought. I entered in,
    And climbed at once the narrow winding stair
Which led me to the dark abode of sin—
    A dismal chamber, wretched, poor, and bare.

With noiseless step I trod the darkened room,
    And found myself beside a little bed ;
There, in the silence of the sultry gloom,
    Upon the pillow lay a fair young head.

Bright were the eyes, dilated, restless, wild,
  And in their depths there burned the fever-bale;
In years she looked but little more than child;
  Her cheek, save for one hectic spot, was pale.

A girl in years, but prematurely old,
  Her haggard face showed signs of wasting pain—
Spake of a story sad as e'er was told,
  A heart despairing and a wildered brain.

And was this she whom in the bygone years
  I well had known—a maiden good and pure—
Before her eyes were wet with many tears,
  Or she been caught within a tempter's lure?

Her glance met mine; a sudden cry and shrill,
  As from some hunted thing in deadly fear,
Rang through the room; then all again was still,
  Though lingered yet the echo on the ear.

And then rose up the old familiar days—
  The croft, the village, and the little stream,
Orchards in bloom, green lanes, and quiet ways—
  These came before me as a waking dream.

And Lilian—her parents' joy and pride,
    Fairest in all the country, near or far,—
Had she crept here, her guilty shame to hide,
    Lost in the darkness like a wandering star !

Without a word I sat down by the bed,
    As rapidly ran out life's failing sands ;
I smoothed the pillow for her dying head,
    And gently took in mine her burning hands.

For she had sinned ; and, lost to fame and name,
    And leaving home, became a waif and stray ;
Upon her brow was stamped the brand of shame—
    She wandered forth at night and shunned the day.

I knew her well ; she was a neighbour's child ;
    We played together on the upland lea,
And chased the butterflies on commons wild,
    And sang our songs beneath the spreading tree.

And so my thoughts went wandering o'er the past,
    Musing on all the sorrow and the sin,
"O God !" I cried, " how long is this to last !
    When will the better, brighter time come in ?"

Man !   Come and see the work that thou hast done,
   Matching thy strength against a woman weak ;
Mark well the victory that thou hast won,
   See it in haggard eye and hollow cheek.

Here in this soul God's image didst thou mar,
   Betraying love, and innocence, and trust ;
Leaving behind a stain, an unhealed scar ;
   Laying its glory even with the dust.

I turned, as low she moaned with labouring breath—
   The death-sweat stood in drops upon her brow ;
Her face was white and wan as ghastly death—
   Horror and anguish held it fully now.

" Lost ! Lost ! " she cried, " Lost ! Lost ! " and sobbed
       and wept,
   And wrung her faded hands, and raised her eyes ;
A shudd'ring tremor o'er her slowly crept,
   And shook her bosom with a storm of sighs.

I spake low words of comfort and of hope ;
   Of One who on the Cross for sin sufficed,
Whose grace with all her guiltiness could cope,
   And magnified the boundless love of Christ.

Oh, never did a hopeless, drowning wretch,
 Sinking beneath the overwhelming wave,
More eagerly a dying hand outstretch
 To clutch the rope which grasped might fully save.

Thus caught she at the tender loving word
 I.breathed with yearnings in her hungry ear ;
Once and again she cried, " O Lord, good Lord !
 Jesu, have mercy ; a poor outcast hear ! "

" And may I take," she said, " such sweet relief,
 And may I, can I, hope to be forgiven ? "
I gently whispered of the dying thief
 Who from a cross stepped up at once to heaven.

" And such the matchless grace for thee," I said,
 " No need is there that even thou despair ; "
At which she meekly bowed a lowly head,
 While trembled on her lips an earnest prayer.

A light came to her restless, fevered eye—
 The flushed and troubled face at once grew calm ;
Peace took the place of stormy agony,
 And o'er the tortured spirit shed its balm.

But still the rapid death-march beat apace,
  Through every quivering pulse and through her blood;
I saw the shadows steal across her face,
  As by her bed, in silent prayer, I stood.

I marked the coming change on cheek and brow,
  I heard the moan, the catchings of the breath;
The bitter fight was being fought out now,
  And to that room had come dread ruthless death.

A sudden start: a low but thrilling cry:
  Upon the face a quivering gleam of light:
Methought I heard the sound quick rushing by
  As of a liberated spirit's flight.

Then all was still. A silence filled the room,
  And ended was the long and painful strife;
Another soul had gone to meet its doom—
  From out the world had passed another life.

THE LOCUST-EATEN YEARS.

" And I will restore to you the years that the locust hath eaten."—
JOEL ii. 25.

WORDS of wonder! What! restore the past,
   Renew the olden days, the happy times,
   The joys and pleasures that fled all too fast,
The hours that struck sweet music from their chimes?

Restore the trust in man that once we knew,
   When no suspicion chilled or slew our love,
And all we met were good, and pure, and true,
   Clear as the wave that glasses heaven above?

Restore the hope that threw a tender light
   O'er the near future, and the distant years,
When life was full of fresh and sweet delight,
   And held no hint of grief or bitter tears?

Restore full-hearted love, which knew not yet
   That coldness can repay affection's smile ;
That lips can lightly promise, and forget
   That 'neath the honeyed words lie cruel guile ?

Oh, can it be, and shall I stand once more
   In the full light of childhood's early spring,
When every hour some fresh enjoyment bore,
   And sang the heart as birds in May-time sing ?

Can even God to us the past restore,
   Or cause the withered flower again to bloom,
The locust-eaten years give back once more,
   Renewing joys long buried in the tomb ?

'Tis even so—He can give back the years
   By locusts eaten, fretted by the worm ;
Can make us reap in joy who sowed in tears ;
   Can bring tranquillity from out the storm.

The barren wastes shall blossom all with flowers,
   And roses spring from out the arid sands :
Bright suns shall shine, and fall the tender showers,
   And verdure crown with beauty all the lands.

Fear not ; the floors shall all be full of wheat,
 The fats shall overflow with ruddy wine,
And for the bitter God shall give the sweet,
 And for the earthly grant us the Divine.

Let us not cast regretful looks behind,
 Rather believe God will the past restore,
That when we enter heaven we shall find,
 The years are ours again for evermore.

F

HOW SHOULD I LIKE TO DIE?

OW should I like to die? you ask; and where?
   Well, I will try to give an answer true;
    I have not made these questions much my care—
They have not troubled me; Friend, have they you?

How would I die?   Not in a far-off land,
   'Mid faces strange, and voices all unknown;
No, let me feel the touch of friendly hand;
   I fain would fall asleep anear mine own.

For it were sweet to die 'mongst those loved best,
   The true, the tender, and the near and dear;
To lay my dying head upon their breast,
   And have their kindly voices in my ear.

Pleasant to see, down-bending from above,
   Affection's yearning gaze, and on it dwell;
To pass away 'mid looks and tones of love;
   To catch the words of low and fond farewell.

Where would I die?   I would the call might come
    'Mid old familiar scenes and cherished ties;
In some dear chamber of the hallowed home,
    There would I close on earth my dying eyes.

When earthly lights are burning dim and low,
    And earthly faces fade from out my sight,
And earthly voices faintly come and go,
    And round me gather shadows of the night—

I then would rest my last and parting gaze
    On things and persons known to me of yore.
Who made the sweetness of the happy days
    When all the hours some pleasure to me bore.

So would I calmly pass from earth away,
    When life is wearing to the welcome ev'n,
Falling asleep, to wake when dawns the day,
    And find myself with Christ in home and heav'n.

KING DAVID.

P and down his lonely chamber
 Paced the King with breaking heart,
Struggling with a hopeless sorrow,—
 Like a stricken deer, apart ;

Wan his face, and very haggard—
 Furrowed all his brow with care ;
Great drops stood upon his forehead ;
 From his eyes stared grim despair.

Wrung he sore his hands in anguish,
 Whilst the tears fell thick and fast,
And his manly frame was shaken
 Like a reed before the blast.

Oft in faltering broken accents,
 Which betrayed a soul undone,
Raising weeping eyes to heaven,
 Wailed he out, "My son ! my son !"

"Absalom, my own, my dear one,
   Dearer than all sons to me ;
Absalom, my loved and lost one,
   Would that I had died for thee !"

Thus he sobbed forth his deep sorrow,
   Moaning ever, moaning low ;
All the spirit torn and tortured
   With the greatness of his woe.

Where were now the fascination,
   Glories of the hair and face,
All the grace and all the glamour,
   Pride of honour, pomp of place ?

Dimmed the splendour and the beauty,
   Sullied, faded, soiled, brought low ;
On his lips the seal of silence,
   Death's cold hand upon his brow.

In that grief so wild and piteous,
   Did the King recall his shame ?
Did no thought of foul transgression
   Scorch and scathe his soul like flame ?

Passed before his mind the murder,
　　Dead Uriah's bloody grave;
How, by craft and cruel counsel,
　　He was slain the true and brave?

Thought he how his guilty passion
　　Struck at honour, name, and fame:
Wrought the husband's dark undoing,
　　And Bath-Shua's utter shame?

Through his weeping and his mourning
　　Thrilled no voice upon his ear,
Like the trump of judgment sounding,
　　Shaking all his soul with fear?

Ah, what mem'ries wrung his spirit,
　　Desolate, bereft, undone,
Forced that cry of desolation—
　　"Absalom, my son! my son!"

For again the Prophet's judgment,
　　Terrible, intrepid, calm,
Smote with fear the quailing monarch,
　　Robber of the poor man's lamb.

Now he sees the flashing aspect,
  Hears once more the damning ban,
As the Seer brands the sinner,
  " Thou, O David, art the man ! "

But the climax of his anguish,
  Torture added to his pain,
Was the deed of dark rebellion
  In which Absalom was slain.

Absalom, the loved and cherished,
  Nearest, dearest to his heart,
Traitor to his crown and kingdom !
  —This it was that barbed the dart.

Was there hope for one so guilty,
  Cut off reckless in his sin ?
Would for him God's heaven open ?
  Could such sinner enter in ?

This the crown of all his sorrow ;
  Ah, this left him woe-begone,
Wrung that cry of sore bereavement,
  " Absalom, my son ! my son ! "

In this world where woe and sadness
　Are but as a common thing,
Grief for life gone out in darkness,
　Has than all a fiercer sting.

Ah, no pang is half so poignant,
　Sorrow greater there is none,
Than beside a hopeless death-bed,
　To wail out, "My son ! my son !"

Then the racked and tortured spirit,
　Musing on the dark to be,
Sobs aloud in piteous angish,
　" Would God I had died for thee !"

CHRIST AT THE DOOR.

THE night had drawn her dusky veil
     O'er all the landscape far and nigh,
   And in the heavens the moonlight pale
      Shed lustre from the solemn sky.
The world was wrapped in slumber deep,
Save where a mourner waked to weep.

Who is it knocks at yonder door,
   His face so strangely sweet and fair,
Standing and knocking evermore,
   With urgent hand and tender air?
A crown of thorns is on His head;
His eyes are full of tears unshed.

Wet are His locks with dews of night;
   The eager winds blow cold and chill;
But in His eyes there burns the light
   Of love that overcometh ill.

Patient, untired, He waits before
That long-closed, barred, and bolted door.

The latch is rusted, and the way
    Is all o'ergrown with thorns and weeds ;
Dark are the panels, stained and grey,
    And here the canker-worm feeds.
All so neglected and forlorn,
That one might pass it by in scorn.

It is the Saviour at the door,
    Wooing the sullen soul behind,
Who in His pity doth implore
    That He an entrance there may find.
" Open," He cries, " poor soul, to Me ;
I will come in and sup with thee.

" Behold, I stand, I stand and knock—
    Open, dear heart, and let me in ;
Wilt thou My mercy scorn and mock,
    For siren laughter, lust, and sin ?
Dreary the night, the dawn is late ;
Ah ! must I here for ever wait ?

" Through days of heat, and days of cold,
    Through nights all wild and dark and chill,
I stand as I have stood of old,
    Seeking to overcome thy will.
Lo, here I am ; I knock again ;
Let not this knocking be in vain.

" 'Tis love alone that keeps Me here,
    Blessings to thee that I may bring ;
Open, there is no cause for fear ;
    I'll make thy very heart to sing.
Receive Me as thy friend, and rest
Shall fill and flood thy weary breast.

" And then when in the days to come,
    The world has passed and time is o'er,
Thou seekest entrance to My home,
    And standest knocking at My door,
Then will I open unto thee,
And thou shalt ever live with Me.

" A royal banquet shall be thine,
    A feast of bliss that cannot cloy :

The bread of God, and heaven's own wine,
   Whate'er can fill thy soul with joy.
Open, dear soul, the long-closed door,
And I am thine for evermore."

COMPLETED JOY.

OF all the words that fill the ear with gladness,
   And like rich treasure in the heart we hide,
Of all the promises that banish sadness,
   What passes this, " I shall be satisfied " ?

What satisfied ?   The soul's immortal longing ;
   The thirsting for the good, the true, the right ;
The vast desires that come upon us thronging ;
   The hungering for knowledge and for light ?

Shall there no wish be ever on us growing,
   That ours were service pure as saints' above ?
No wish : since we are filled to overflowing
   With all the fulness of the Godhead's love.

O blessed hope ; hope that no more for ever
   Desires unsatisfied shall vex the soul ;
That yearnings unfulfilled shall trouble never
   The peace of those that reach the heavenly goal.

I cannot tell the glories of that heaven
   Where God in Christ, and Christ in God, is all ;
Where burn the lamps, the mystic wondrous Seven,
   And saints in lowly adoration fall.

Enough for hearts weary of sin and sorrow,
   And still athirst when earthly streams are tried,
Enough that soon shall dawn that glorious morrow
   When we, awaking, shall be satisfied.

No longer then bewildered by false seemings,
   The substance shall be ours, the shadow gone ;
Beguiled no longer by unstable dreamings,
   We from the dark shall pass into the sun.

Here, then, I rest at peace, all doubtings over ;
   " Here," can I say, " I will with joy abide ; "
No bliss beyond this wish I to discover ;
   Enough for me, " I shall be satisfied."

THE SLEEP.

SHE is not dead.   She only lies a sleeping,
    Her dear head pillowed on her Saviour's
      breast ;
  Then why this wringing of the hands and
    weeping ?
  There is no cause for tears ; she is at rest.

She is at rest from all the pain and sorrow,
  The cares and roughness of the toilsome way,
The doubts, the anxious fears about the morrow,
  The burning heat and burden of the day.

Our God has called her to Himself in heaven,
  And set her full within that perfect light,
Where morning never darkens into even,
  Where noon ne'er waning fades into a night.

Her voice is no more tuned to notes of sadness,
　　But lifts itself in sweet and holy psalm;
Her face is all alight with wondering gladness,
　　Her hand is waving the victorious palm.

O happy spirit, happy now for ever!
　　More bless'd than thought conceives, or tongue can
　　　　tell,
The chilling winds of grief shall reach thee never,
　　Round thee no tempests rage, nor billows swell.

Nor art thou lost; for when our Christ shall gather
　　His ransomed round Him on the sapphire floor,
When He presents them all unto the Father,
　　Thou shalt be ours again for evermore.

Sweet sleep of death! and oh, the sweet awaking
　　Within the arms of everlasting love!
Oh, smile of God upon Thy children breaking,
　　To bid them welcome to the home above!

She is not dead; she only lies a sleeping,
　　With eyelids closed, hands folded on her breast;
Hush thy sad cries, restrain thy bitter weeping,
　　Life's toil is over, and she is at rest.

GOD'S CHASTENINGS.

SHRINK not from sorrows; 'tis not wise—
They are but mercies in disguise;
Ladders by which we mount and rise.

"Ministering spirits," they are sent
As Angels from God's firmament,
On heavenly messages intent.

Take them in love; in love they come,
To call our heart to that fair home
From which it is so prone to roam.

Learn from each grief its lesson true,
What God would have thee think and do,
What path avoid, or road pursue.

Whate'er betide, whate'er befall,
Be very sure there's love in all;
Love, though it fret, and wound, and gall

G

For thus, through trouble, shame, and loss,
By many a bitter pang and cross,
He would refine and purge the dross.

Look then on sorrow as a friend ;
Rough means unto a gracious end ;
As on the heavenly way you wend.

You cry to God that He would spare,
The wintry days and bitter air,
The wasting trouble and the care.

You long for pastures green and still,
The sheltered way, the gentle rill,
The summer days, the wooded hill.

Yet winter has its use, and frost ;
Without them many a hope were crost ;
The golden harvest spoiled and lost.

They kill the noxious worm, the weed,
And baneful creatures that would feed
Upon the precious buried seed.

Thus trial is a wholesome thing ;
Though sharpest grief our hearts may wring,
It doth with it a blessing bring.

Give it fair welcome ; all God's ways
Will call forth endless strains of praise,
Throughout the long eternal days.

THE SORROWFUL SEA.

THERE is a sorrow on the sounding sea,
  A trouble ever heaving in its breast,
A wail as from a soul in agony,
    An undertone of wild and sad unrest.

The waves break mournfully upon the shore,
  Or surge in fitful fury 'gainst the rock ;
Anon retreat with melancholy roar,
  Tortured and torn, and writhing from the shock.

What hear we in that sorrowful sea-moan ?
  A dirge-like voice, a sound of hoarse farewells,
Despair that lurks in ev'ry hollow tone,
  Sadder than requiem rung from funeral bells.

I catch the cry of storm-tossed men from far,
  A shriek of wrecked ones thrilling 'cross the deep
Rising to God upward from star to star,
  As cruel waters o'er the drowning sweep.

Courage and youth no pity have from thee,
　Nor hope a spell to tame thy heartless might ;
Prayer cannot charm thee, oh thou cruel sea !
　Nor love o'ercome thee in the dreadful fight.

When will thy waves in tranquil stillness lie ?
　The sorrow in thy heart for ever cease ?
And the loud clash of tempests pass and die
　Into the harmony of endless peace ?

The earth lies quiet like a child asleep :
　The deep heart of the heaven is calm and still,
Must thou alone a restless vigil keep,
　And with thy sobbing all the silence fill ?

The wail of sorrow rising from thy breast
　Tells of a hidden and a nameless pain ;
Will nothing soothe that anguish into rest,
　So that it never, never wake again ?

O God, bring Thou the promised happy time
　Which is to bless the ages yet to be ;
Ring in with bells of heav'n's own sweetest chime
　The golden year when "shall be no more sea."

MISERERE, DOMINE!

ESU, Thy mercy we implore,
    The tempest swells, the winds are high,
The troubled waters chafe and roar,
And clouds are darkening o'er the sky.
    As suppliants we come to Thee ;
    Miserere, Domine !

O Thou that on the bitter cross
    Did'st bleed and die for human sin,
Content to suffer pain and loss
    If man's redemption Thou might'st win ;
    To Thee for refuge, Lord, we flee ;
    Miserere, Domine !

Oh ! fold us, Saviour, 'neath Thy wing,
    Oh ! shield us in Thy gracious love,
Around us Thy broad shadows fling,
    And watch us from Thy heaven above ;
    Our Guardian and Protector be ;
    Miserere, Domine !

Once Thou didst hush the angry wind,
   And lull the waves in tranquil sleep;
The tempest's fury Thou didst bind,
   To show Thy power upon the deep;
      Didst Thou not walk the stormy sea?
      Miserere, Domine!

Then hold us safe within Thy hand,
   And bring us to the farther shore;
We fain would reach that happy land
   Where storms will threaten never more.
      We have no hope, Lord, but in Thee;
      Miserere, Domine!

THE CHALLENGE TO THE SWORD.

"O thou sword of the Lord, how long will it be ere thou be quiet?
Put up thyself into thy scabbard; rest, and be still."—JER.
xlvii. 6.

SWORD of the Lord, wilt thou never be still?
How long wilt thou flash to destroy and to kill?
Return to the scabbard: rest, rest in the sheath!
Wilt thou never have done with the dark work of death?

O sword of the Lord, must the shriek rend the air,
The cry of the widow and child in despair?
Must the vineyard be wasted, the field trampled down,
And the festering dead choke the streets of the town?

Wilt thou never be sated with blood of the slain,
The moans of their anguish, their wounds, and their
  pain?
Are the harvests this green earth is ever to yield
Red harvests reaped down in the fierce battlefield?

Sick at heart with thy triumphs, we ask thee how long
Wilt thou mow down the young, and the brave, and the
    strong?
Are War's carnage and carnival never to cease?
Shall the world never bask in the sunshine of peace?

O sword of the Lord, sharp, furbished, and keen,
Thou art drunk with the blood of the slaughtered, I
    ween;
End, end, and for ever, the strife and the pain,
And the battle that hurtles aloud on the plain.

Rest, rest in thy scabbard; rust, rust in thy sheath;
Cease at last to lay low the thick swathes of death;
Sleep, if but for a season; be quiet, be still;
Of anguish and blood thou hast more than thy fill.

Let it break, the glad day by prophets foretold,
When earth shall rejoice in the bright age of gold;
When the din of the conflict for ever is o'er,
And nation shall rise against nation no more!

Then the sword to a share shall be beaten and turned,
The spear to a pruning-hook, the battle-axe burned;
Then the use of the drum and the trumpet shall cease,
Or sound but to herald the long reign of peace.

THE CHALLENGE ANSWERED.

*" How can it be quiet, seeing the Lord hath given it a charge against
Ashkelon, and against the sea-shore? there hath He appointed
it."—Jer. xlvii. 7.*

" OW *can* it be quiet," this sword of the Lord?
  God has spoken in judgment and given the
   word;
'Tis He who unsheathes it, 'tis He sends it forth,
Grim and ghastly, to deal with the nations of earth.

" How can it be quiet?" The charge has been given
To take its keen blade and " bathe it in heaven;"
For the crimes that are daily relentlessly done,
Call it forth from the scabbard to flash in the sun.

God has sent it in doom 'gainst the sea-shore of pride,
'Gainst Ashkelon's sins in their full-breasted tide;
So it holds ever on in its terrible path,
Bearing with it the sign of the Holy One's wrath.

" Quiet ! " What, when the wailings of grief and despair,
The sighings of sorrow are filling the air ;
When such wrongs and such horrors through Christendom
    sweep,
As cause devils to laugh, and good angels to weep !

" Quiet ! " What, when dark hotbeds of vice curse each
    town,
When the rich men are boasting, the poor trodden down,
When sedition and murder are stalking abroad,
And men are blaspheming the name of their God !

" Quiet ! " What, when the cries of disease and of pain,
Rise from hearts that are breaking, again and again,
When folly and passion, ambition and strife,
Are killing all hope in full many a life !

The stern sword of the Lord on its mission must go,
And the record of earth be one burden of woe,
War's tocsin must sound, ay, and thousands be slain,
And crimsoned with blood be the fair harvest plain.

It will not be quiet, nor rest evermore,
Till the Light shall arise and the darkness be o'er ;
Till tyranny ceases, cruel bigotry, lust,
And God's enemies lie at His feet in the dust.

When the sword has fulfilled the stern charge of the Lord,
And accomplished the righteous behests of His word,
When have passed from the world the dark shadows of ill,
'Twill return to the scabbard, 'twill rest and be still.

Patience yet for a while, and then all will be well,
Sin and death shall be bound in their own native hell;
The Saviour shall claim the whole world for His own,
And on earth shall establish His kingdom and throne.

FROM THE DUST.

Y soul fast cleaveth to the dust,
    My heart within is dead and cold,
    I'm blown about by every gust,
    No certain anchorage I hold.
I fain would lift mine eyes on high,
But all unpurged they cannot see ;
I feel like one about to die ;
Have mercy, Jesu, quicken me !

My life is like the untilled land,
On which no flower or fruitage grows ;
'Tis like a waste of arid sand,
A wintry landscape clothed with snows.
All empty are the vanished years ;
Shall like the past the future be ?
'Gainst this I plead with prayers and tears,
Have mercy, Jesu, quicken me !

My life is like to plants that creep,
Like plants that droop and touch the ground ;
No seed I sow, no harvest reap,
All barren as the months go round.
Uproot me then, and plant again,
I would be fruitful unto thee ;
Prune, cleanse me, Lord, I'll scorn the pain :
Have mercy, Jesu, quicken me !

IN MEMORIAM, W. D. CREWDSON,

DIED DECEMBER 2, 1878.

LIFE of holiness, whose end was Christ ;
   A steadfast gaze upon the things unseen ;
Suff'ring borne patiently, for God sufficed ;
   Crowned by a death calm, beautiful, serene.

So close his walk and intercourse with God,
   Such converse ever held he with this Friend,
That, as he trod the straight and narrow road,
   He seemed at times in heaven before the end.

His face was as an angel's, bright with love,
   Through which the saintly spirit shone out clear ;
So much he lived amongst the things above,
   He caught a beauty from the upper sphere.

For overflowings of the light within
   So lit, as with a fire, his kindling eye,
He looked like one already passed from sin
   To the pure glories of the stainless sky.

Gazing through tears upon the brow so calm,
   We asked in wonder, " What ! can this be death ? "
Not death ; he lived to chant the new sweet psalm
   To which, while here, God had attuned his breath.

A smile still lingered on the dear white face,
   A solemn majesty was o'er it spread ;
On cheek and brow a holy, tender grace,
   That lent pathetic beauty to the dead.

No longer ached the heart, nor throbbed the brain ;
   Nor pain nor sorrow troubled now his breast ;
For him " clear was the shining after rain,"
   His peace unbroken, and profound his rest.

Friends came to look their last on one so dear,
   Who in their loving hands sweet flowers did bring,
And laid them tenderly upon the bier,
   Where gleamed the words, " Gone in to see the King."

WHAT IS YOUR LIFE?

MAN'S life is but a shadowy, fleeting vapour,
  That quickly melts and vanishes away ;
  'Tis like a cloud which gathers in the morning,
  And passes, ere dawn deepens into day.

But shall this thought bring with it any sorrow,
  Or fill our hearts with a regretful grief ?
Shall it cast shadow on the coming morrow,
  To know this human life is all so brief ?

What ! shall we idly fold our hands before us,
  Mourning the stern, inexorable doom ?
Or shall we spend our days in pining sadness,
  Because we hasten surely to the tomb ?

What ! shall we grow all mad and wild and reckless,
  Ready to utter this despairing cry :
" Let us take our ease, and eat, drink, and be merry,
  For on the morrow we are sure to die " ?

No, never ! For the thought will rather urge us,
  To work with both hands earnestly for God !
We will be up and doing in His service,
  If all so soon we lie beneath the sod.

A vapour ! Yes ; but let us all remember,
  The vapour gives its beauty to the air ;
It drapes the skies in crimson, blue, and amber,
  And shapes itself in cloudlets bright and fair.

Then we will turn our brief life to a glory,
  And make it beautiful with deeds of love ;
Yes, we will steep it in the dyes of heaven,
  And colour it with light caught from above.

A vapour ! Yes ; but 'tis not therefore worthless ;
  Vapour condensed is changed into the steam
Which sends the vessel o'er the trackless ocean,
  And drives with speed the sounding iron team.

If life be brief, we will be more in earnest,
  And work for God with all our soul and might ;
Running with girded loins the race before us,
  Fighting with all our strength the noble fight.

So when to heaven is drawn the earthly vapour,
  And we are called to stand before the throne,
The Master's smile shall form our happy guerdon,
  And we shall hear Him say, " Well done ! Well done ! "

EVER WITH GOD.

" When I awake, I am still with Thee."—PSALM cxxxix. 18.

HEN sinks the sun far in the glimmering west,
  And shadows lengthen over field and fell,
    I lay me down in peace and take my rest,
      For Thou in safety, Lord, dost make me dwell.

Thou drawest round the curtains of the night,
  And sendest sleep to close my heavy eyes,
Keeping true watch, until the morning light
  Reddens the east and steals along the skies.

Meanwhile, within the Everlasting Arms,
  Which underneath me lovingly are spread,
I rest secure with Thee from all that harms ;
  Thy breast a pillow for my weary head.

Sweet is the sleep o'ershadowed by Thy love,
  Sweeter the dreams all brightened by Thy grace ;
All heaven appears descending from above,
  When I in visions see Thy glorious face.

And when the dayspring ripples o'er the lawn,
  When pipes the early bird in bush and tree,
And dewdrops turn to diamonds in the dawn,
  When I awake, Lord, I am still with Thee.

" With Thee !" this is my first and earliest thought ;
  " With Thee!" this in my heart finds latest place;
" With Thee !" the consciousness with joy is fraught ;
  I sleep to wake within Thy sweet embrace.

So shall it be in that, the last long sleep,
  When I am laid within my narrow bed,
Thou wilt a tender watch upon me keep,
  For precious in Thy sight are all Thy dead.

And when the Easter morning breaks the gloom,
  And death and darkness shall for ever flee,
Triumphant rising from the yawning tomb
  I shall awake, to know " I'm still with Thee."

ON THE

DEATH OF THE REV. HENRY WRIGHT.

(Drowned in Coniston Lake, August 13, 1880.)

IS then the world the sport of chance,
 And under no controlling mind,
 Whirled blindly on by every wind,
Plaything and jest of circumstance?

Are we but driven here and there,
 Like leaves in autumn, sere and dead,
 That lightly strew the ground we tread,
Or idly blown about in air?

Oh cruel irony of life—
 With nothing sure from hour to hour,
 Where lurks the poison 'neath the flower,
And sweetest cup with death is rife;

Where lightnings rend the strongest tree,
 And brightest morn is closed in cloud,
 Where fairest face lies in the shroud,
And hope oft holds despair in fee.

And can it be God feels no pain,
 Seated upon His happy throne,
 As earth's unceasing wail and moan
Rises through all His Angels' strain

To smite His ear with bitter cry,
 To strike it through the Seraphs' songs,
 And jar their music with the wrongs
Of human hearts that break and die ?

Or is it true, as some men tell,
 " Whatever is, is good and right,"
 That in the darkest cloud is light,
And all that happens must be well ?

Why then leave feeble, palsied age,
 A burden to itself and earth,
 And taking all we hold of worth,
Sweep youth and strength from off the stage ?

Must that man, leprous with his sin,
  Live on to vex the ear and eye;
  And he untimely droop and die
Who unto angels was akin?

O God in Heaven! Thou knowest well
  How worse than wasted some lives be,
  Nought ever done for man or Thee,
But rather deeds befitting hell.

Why not from earth take one of these,
  And leave the true souls with us still
  Who strove to do Thy righteous will,
Consulting not for self or ease?

The Husband, Father, Pastor, Friend,
  Loyal in each, to many dear,
  Who kept his spirit pure and clear,
Whose life did always upward tend?

Peace, foolish heart! Look up and rise
  Above the narrow walls of time,
  And with untroubled faith sublime
Consider all with unsealed eyes.

His life, though brief, was not in vain ;
   He lived to do some noble deeds,
   He lived to sow some precious seeds
Which shall bear fruit in ripened grain.

Rich benedictions oft he had
   For kindly deeds, and thoughtful care,
   And children's love, the poor man's prayer,
With blessings of the sick and sad.

God reckons not our life by days,
   Rather by all we live to do,
   By hours redeemed for all things true,
Things just and worthy of all praise.

To doubt is sin—God reigns on high,
   Above the sorrow and the strife,
   Above this dark, mysterious life,
And hears our helpless human cry.

To doubt is wrong—Our God is Love,
   Although His ways are hid from sight,
   Although in vain we search for light,
And in the deep His footsteps move.

A PORTRAIT

She took...

- Pope

Let tavern-keepers curse and brawl,
    And men the poisoned chalice drain,
    That fires the heart, and dulls the brain,
And turns the sweets of life to gall.

Oh, rich men say if it is good
    The poor should herd in crowded rooms,
    'Mid stagnant air, and stifling glooms,
Where vices thrive, and fevers brood?

Who holds "'tis right" that ghastly war
    Should raise on high its flaming torch,
    To light men on their horrid march,
God's stamp in other men to mar?

Right is it thus in carnage dread,
    To redden harvest fields with blood,
    Forgetful of the holy rood,
And Prince of Peace that hung there dead?

Shall hearts and homes with sorrow shake,
    Because for cruel greed of gain,
    The lightning-wingèd iron train
Should lack the life-preserving brake?

And what of vessels sent to sea,
   Unfit to battle with the wave ;
   Mann'd with the gallant and the brave,
Men doomed by Mammon's stern decree ?

Is't right to bow at wealth's proud shrine ?
   That all be counted loss for gold ?
   Daughters in marriage-market sold,
To drink love's lees, and not its wine ?

Think of the frauds that curse the mart,
   The lies that circulate on 'Change,
   The wrongs that through our system range,
And sores that fester at the heart.

And are these "right" ?   Are they of God ?
   Does He look down on them and smile,
   Approving hate, and lust, and guile,
Or does He not restrain the rod ?

Statesmen that hold their country's good,
   Less than their own poor selfish aims,
   Lower than low ambition's claims—
Suits this the philosophic mood ?

" Whatever is, is right," you say,
    Oh coward creed, and born of sloth,
    And empty as the bubble-froth,
Blown by an infant at its play !

Alas ! on all sides thrives the wrong ;
    Then, let us up, and 'gainst it fight,
    Resolved God's foes and man's to smite,
Like Jael in the old-world song.

Thus if we do upon our way
    To hopes that crown the eternal years,
    Harvests that spring from seeds of tears,
Shall be reaped down in God's own day.

Not ours to say, " What is, is right ;"
    'Tis God's with good to vanquish ill,
    To make all things work out His will,
And on the darkness shed the light.

MISCELLANEOUS.

THE CONVENT GRATE.

WHAT, will he never, never come?
 I sent to him an hour ago.
 I cannot bear the madd'ning strain,
The fires within me that consume,
The torture, agony, and pain,
The horror of the coming tomb.
These old men are so slow—so slow!
The day is wearing on to eve,
The last that I shall ever see—
He would not mock me or deceive.
If I could break these prison bars,
Through which I hardly see the stars,
To him all quickly would I flee,
And pour into his awe-struck ear
My tale of sin, to lay all bare
My heart, my soul, its shame and fear;
These, these before my conscience glare,
And drive and goad me to despair.

         I

I long denied and cloaked it all,
My heart was hard as this cold stone
'Gainst which I press my aching breast
To still its throbbings into rest.
I did not even make a moan,
Nor sob, nor utter any cry,
Not when I found myself alone;
No, not a tear was in my eye,
Although I saw her bleeding fall,
And felt and knew that she would die.
But now I am no longer brave;
My heart is filled with bitter dread;
I know they've dug for me a grave—
I long my soul to purge and save;
To-morrow sees me with the dead.
But hark! Ah, surely this is he
Who comes to shrive my guilty soul.
I hear the key turn in the door;
How shall I tell my bitter dole,
Lay bare my crime, reveal my woe?
Yet all shall be confessed by me.
I hear his step upon the floor—
Father! father! thou art come!
I will no more, no more be dumb,

Thou shalt know all, all, all.
Yes ; I am guilty ! do not shrink,
Oh ! do not turn away thy face ;
Have mercy, father ; show some grace—
I stand upon the icy brink
Of death ; I know my fate, my doom—
The rack, the torture ! Save me, save !
If that thou canst. I do repent.
Oh ! must I leave the prison's gloom
To meet the headsman's cruel eye !
Beneath his glittering axe to die,
Then thrown into the loathsome grave !
Is there no hope they will relent ?
Father, I turn to you with tears ;
I am so young—my mother dead—
No one to care for me or lead ;
A child, a foolish child in years.
Listen again. I see your eyes
Are yearning towards me. Ah, you feel
For me. I hear your sighs ;
Your heart is human—'tis not steel ;
It is not death I so much dread,
If there were rest when I am dead.
Ah, to lay down my head to sleep

On earth's calm breast, no more to weep,
Or waken to another morn
To face man's cruel hate and scorn !
Ah, this were blessed, this were sweet !
But oh, to think that I must meet
The Judge upon the Judgment Seat !
I dread His wrath—I fear His ire—
The deathless worm—the quenchless fire ;
Save me from these, the curse, the ban,
Save me, dear Father, if you can !
Yes, I will tell you all.—Bend down
Your ear, and do not shrink or start ;
Take pity on me ; do not frown,
As I lay bare to thee my heart.
Young Giuglio,—I remember not
The time when we were not as one.
Our homes were near, among the vines—
To grow together was our lot.
We played as children in the sun,
We worked together in the shade,
We sat together neath the pines,
We knelt together, and we prayed ;
And in San Joseph's solemn aisle,
Heard what the holy father said,

When speaking of the joys of heaven,
How men repent and are forgiven.
We loved, loved truly, without guile.
I hardly knew a mother's love—
I was an infant when she died,
And she was taken up above
To rest with God in Paradise,
Far from my wistful heart and eyes,
And, from my weeping father's side.
For me, I was left near alone,
And did what pleased me,—worked or played,
Wandered by valley, stream, and glade,
And so grew up.   Some called me fair,
And praised the lustre of my hair.
I cared not for their praise or blame,
One only did I seek to please—
Others to me were all the same ;
But Giuglio, oh my love, my life !
My Morning-Star, my joy, my light !
Sweet as the breezes of the May ;
He was to make me his own wife—
To keep me ever in his sight,
And be mine own strong staff and stay.
And so for me the world grew bright,

More sweet the day ; more fair the night.
The world was like a Paradise,
From which there rose a happy hymn,
And angels from the heavens looked down
With kind and sympathising eyes.
And I was seated on a throne,
And queen-like reigned in bliss alone,
Crowned with my Giuglio's happy love,
A crown to me all crowns above.
I must not linger on the joy,
The bliss was brief.   A serpent came
Into my garden,—brought a curse,
It wore a woman's face,—was fair,
Had fatal beauty to destroy ;
Black browed, with eyes of subtle flame,
And glorious clouds of purple hair,
With meshes to ensnare the soul.
She had a cold and cruel smile,
False, false, and fitted to beguile.
She caught my Giuglio in her snare.

His love from me she slowly stole,
And made him her poor foolish slave,
Drawing him surely by her art.
The world for me became a grave,

Wherein lay buried my dead heart,
And over which she lightly trod.
She triumphed when she saw me sad—
I was to her but as the sod
On which she placed her dainty feet.
Her scorn, her laughter, made me mad.
The sunshine left my darkened life,
'Twas all o'ershadowed with a cloud.
I withered 'neath the inward strife;
I longed to wear the deathly shroud,
That all the passion and the fever
Might pass, for ever and for ever,
And I low in the ground, at rest,
The green grass waving o'er my breast.
Oh, to have died there at his feet!
That would have been most sweet, most sweet.
But death was not so to be won—
I was to live, live sadly on,
When all that made life dear was gone.
The days passed by, I know not how,
I could not say if summer shone,
Or winter came with chilling snow—
My heart was dead, and still, and cold—
My face grew pinched, and grey, and wan—

And youth was o'er, and I was old.
My life became a wintry thing—
For me there was no future spring.
One evening late I walked alone,
My heart hard, lifeless as a stone ;
And through the garden passed, and by
The thick-leafed vines, and through the flowers
Which scented all the dusky air,
I paused a moment with a sigh—
All was so sweet and fragrant there.
Father, I think I smell them now,
Jasmine, and rose, and lily fair.
Then heard I voices, saw them pace
The twilight alleys, up and down.
Love looked from out his up-turned face,
And set upon her head a crown.
He drew her dainty hand in his,
She leaned against him all her weight,
He stooped and gave her one long kiss—
And I was forced to see their bliss.
I, that stood there so desolate,
I heard her laugh a silver laugh,
It pierced me like a sharpened sword,
It ran like fire through all my blood,

It maddened me as there I stood,
A devil it within me stirred—
It was too sweet,—too sweet by half.
I looked on—stricken, wounded, slain,
With tortured heart and whirling brain.
Father, would'st know what then took place?
They walked together to the door,
I followed through the dusky gloom,
Drawn by a fatal secret force
That held and pressed me more and more,
And drew me onward to my doom.
With heart aflame and ghastly face,
I saw them part with fond embrace,
And then he left her. She went in—
I glided swiftly after her.
She turned; she saw me where I stood;
She smiled the smile of those who sin.
I for a moment did not stir,
And then in wild and wrathful mood
I spoke; she answered, laughed; and then
I felt the dagger 'neath my breast;
Held it a moment tightly pressed;
And as I heard the laugh again
That stung me with a sudden pain,

I raised my hand,—there shrilled a cry,
Upon her dress I saw a stain ;
'Twas blood, red blood ; I know the why—
The dagger ! Yes, close to my heart,
Hidden beneath my dress it lay ;
But why I kept it closely there,
I hardly know or cannot say.
Perhaps that it might give me rest,
And save me from my dark despair.
Father, I think that I was mad—
I left the house ; I did not care
What next befell. Why should I flee,
For what was left of life to me ?
'Tis all confused what happened then ;
A crowd of faces ; startling cries ;
Women aghast and wondering men ;
My father, horror in his eyes,
Their lids all red with unshed tears ;
And Giuglio with a face like stone,
White, as the dead, with such a look
Of woe, as though had passed whole years
And left him old. His whole frame shook
And trembled like the aspen leaf,
And in his eyes, as in a book,

I read my guilt. And then a swoon
Brought for a season sweet relief.
Oh, never to have waked again !
That in death's arms I might have lain !
The waking came too soon, too soon,
I woke, and found me here. The rest
You know. Father, I am to die—
To-morrow ? Is it then so near ?
Only a summer night between
Me and the bitter doom I fear?
A few more hours,—what shall have been ?
Can it indeed be then so soon ?
Shall I not see again that moon
Which shineth brightly through these bars,
Nor look upon those happy stars,
Nor move amongst the fragrant flowers,
Nor train again the trellised vine ?
No ! I can reckon up the hours
Before they take this life of mine.
Well, let that go. My sin ! my sin !
Can I for this forgiveness win ?
Say, is there hope for me— and where ?
Tell me some refuge from despair.
For oh, to die with this poor hand

All red with blood ! and then to go
And meet with God, where she will be
To charge the guilty deed on me !
For then together we shall stand,
And on my brow will burn the brand
Of murder !   Oh, the woe, the woe,
The deathless worm, the quenchless flame,
The horror, agony, and shame !
Have pity, Father, save, oh save !
Let me not fill a hopeless grave !
" Mary !" the Virgin Mother mild,
The gentle, good, and undefiled,
What, what,—oh, tell me what of her ?
She is too pure, too far above
A wicked, cruel thing like me ;
I am not worthy of her love,
Or tenderness—No, let that be—
For if I prayed she would not hear ;
No cry of mine her heart would move ;
She standeth on the glassy sea,
And songs of angels, sweet and clear,
Fill with their harmonies her ear.
What knows she of the maddened mind,
The tortured heart, the burning brain,

The deep remorse, the gnawing pain,
The fears that all my senses bind,
The horror more than I can tell,
The dread that scorches like a hell?
Speak not of *her*. Tell me of one,
If such there be, who will not scorn
A sinner guilty, lost, undone,
Outcast from all, helpless, forlorn ;
Who will both pity and show grace.
Tell me of such, Father, I pray,
Nay, look not with that hopeless face,
The hours are speeding fast away ;
To me is left but little space
Before the breaking of the day.
And at the dawn—you know the rest.
Ah, lives no pity in your breast?
That Crucifix—you hold it there
Between me and my dark despair,
Truly I trusted to it once
My hope lay in that carvéd bronze.
But now,—nay, Father,—do not start,
I need a living, loving heart ;
His,—His,—I need,—the Man, the Man,
Who died upon the bitter cross,

And mockery and anguish bare,
And shame, and suffering and loss,
And all, and more than nature can ;
Bare it for sinners on the rood—
Ah, He was merciful and good !
I would have nothing pass between
Me and the Christ on whom I lean.
Oh, it were wondrous strange and sweet
To fall like her of old, love-led,
Down at His own dear blessed feet,
And wash them with the tears I shed,
And weep, and weep, till I were dead.
He would not spurn me from the place,
For He was ever full of grace,
And loving, pitiful, and kind.
The lost He came to seek and find ;
The broken heart to heal and bind.
Have mercy, Jesu ; here I lie ;
Low from the dust to Thee I cry ;
No one so lost, undone, as I.
Oh, by Thy seven bleeding wounds,
And by the scars on hands and side,
By shudd'ring wail, and awful sounds,
That pierced the skies from Calvary,

And by the flowing, crimson tide,
Oh, save me, Jesu, or I die!
Hark! Hark! Did'st thou not hear them toll
The great and solemn funeral bell?
'Twas for the passing of my soul
That loudly rang that dismal knell.
Now shrive me—speak the words of peace.
'Tis well. My death is drawing near,
The headsman, he will soon be here—
I hear his steps. Well, let him come;
I am prepared to meet my doom,
Nor think, good Father, I would live;
I shrink no longer from the tomb,
Dark though it be, and full of gloom.
But Giuglio!—pray him to forgive;
And say that I still thought of him,
E'en 'neath the headsman's axe so keen,
And loved him. Say all this from me,
And more,—I hope to meet him, where
In the now near eternity
There is no sin, and no despair.
One moment—kneel with me in prayer—
Now, Father,—let us go.

WILLIAM D'ALBINEY.

A BALLAD.

FAIR England's Knights and Barons brave
   Rose in one noble band,
Their altars and their hearths to save
   From a tyrant's cruel hand.

With fearless hearts resolved they stood
   Their freedom to obtain;
Nor would they, though it cost their blood,
   In serfdom base remain.

King John had trampled on their rights,
   To the winds had flung the oath,
Which, on his faith, he gave his knights,
   Pledging his solemn troth.

And so their men they summoned all
   To join them in the fray;
Ready in such a cause to fall,
   Could they not win the day.

Amongst them was a man of fame,
  A valiant knight and bold ;
William D'Albiney hight his name,
  With a heart as true as gold.

They placed him foremost in command,
  A Captain true and tried,
To lead in fight the noblest band
  In all the country's side.

Then at their head he marchèd down,
  Where Thames doth broadly sweep
By meadow, village, busy town,
  To Rochester's great keep.

The Archbishop held its castle strong,
  A holy man and true,
Who from his soul abhorred the wrong,
  As holy man should do.

And when these trusty knights and brave
  Marched there in warlike state,
Praying that entrance they might have,
  He opened wide the gate.

K

They enter 'neath the archway's gloom,
　　They mount the narrow stair;
And now they know their cruel doom,
　　The place is blank and bare;

For here there are no sheep or beeves
　　To smoke upon the board;
No bread is here; of harvest sheaves
　　There is no golden hoard.

They stand dismayed, they stand aghast,
　　They gaze around in fear;
Has the gate been passed by them at last
　　That they may perish here!

Then murmurs rise, both loud and deep,
　　Hoarse as the ocean's roar
When waters leap with an angry sweep
　　Upon the rock-bound shore.

" Let's quit this cursed niggard place
　　Before it be too late;
Better the foeman's brand to face
　　Than famine be our fate!"

Above the din one voice was heard,
　　It rose and stilled the cry;
D'Albiney's heart with rage was stirred,
　　A fire flashed from his eye.

" What, Knights !   Deserters !   Can it be?
　　Ye will not thus deny
Your manhood and your chivalry !
　　'Twere better far to die."

Soon as his tongue had spake the words
　　Then sharp the war cry rose;
From scabbards leaped the polished swords,
　　Ready to smite their foes.

The town itself shall yield them all
　　That they can wish or need;
They will not leave the city's wall;
　　The Burghers them shall feed.

" Let but D'Albiney lead them forth,"
　　They cry as with one breath,
" To east, or west, or south, or north,
　　They'll follow him to death."

King John when he the tidings hears,
    That Rochester is ta'en,
Swears, by the holy Mother's tears,
    It shall be won again.

And so he marches quickly down
    The city fair to save ;
Blockades the castle and the town,
    With valiant men and brave.

Thick showers of stones and arrows fly,
    Which darken all the air,
Hurled at the castle's ramparts high,
    And the men besiegèd there.

But the gallant knights inside the gate
    All bear themselves right well ;
And if they're doomed by cruel fate,
    Their lives will dearly sell.

'Tis well that they are true of heart,
    And nerved for bloody fight ;
Ready with life and all to part,
    Rather than yield the right ;

For the barons who had pledged their troth
    To help them and their cause,
Who on the Gospels swore an oath
    They would uphold the laws,

And help D'Albiney in his strait,
    And lend to him their aid,
Now leave him, cowards! to his fate;
    The cravens, sore afraid!

He and his men, both one and all,
    Alone defy the foe;
Right gallantly they keep the wall,
    And work the siegers woe.

One day John and a peerless knight,
    In warlike pomp and state,
With armour gleaming in the light,
    Rode to the castle gate.

The knight he bore for noble name
    Savarii de Marleon;
From fields of Brittany he came
    To fight for great King John.

A man with cross-bow in his hand
 Stood on the castle tower;
Best of D'Albiney's noble band,
 Of his body-guard the flower.

Then up he spoke unto his lord,
 Then boldly out spoke he;
And low and earnest was his word,
 But brave and fierce and free.

"Is it thy will, great knight," he said,
 "That I should smite the king?
A word, and John is with the dead,
 By arrow from this string.

The king he is our bitter foe,
 Cruel as death is he;
This arrow, sire, shall lay him low,
 And England shall be free."

He raised the cross-bow up on high,
 Placed arrow on the string;
Full soon the wingèd bolt shall fly,
 To pierce the unconscious king.

But up and spoke D'Albiney now,
   And, oh, he spoke right loud :
And dark as the thunder was his brow,
   Ere it bursts from the riven cloud.

"No, Villain, no ! what ! dost not fear
   To lift unhallowed hand
Against the Lord's anointed here,
   The king of all this land ?

"Forbear, forbear the bloody deed,
   And let the king pass on ;
Though death indeed be tyrants' meed,
   Harm not the royal John."

To him the Villain then did say,
   "This king we must not spare ;
If he should worst us in the fray,
   What deed will he not dare ?"

To whom the knight, with reverent head,
   Did thus at once reply,
"God's will be done !" and then he said,
   "Not thus King John must die."

Like David once, when Israel's king
　　Before him sleeping lay,
D'Albiney scorned to do such thing,
　　Or take his life away ;

But spared the man that was his foe,
　　Nor harmed his sacred head,
Although he might have struck the blow
　　Had laid him with the dead.

But ill King John repaid the knight
　　For this great act of grace ;
With him the might was more than right,
　　So mean his heart, and base.

When famine pressed D'Albiney sore,
　　And hunger gnawed his men,
And e'en the hope itself was o'er
　　That buoyed him up till then.

He did on great St. Andrew's Day
　　A solemn council hold,
Where swarmed, like tigers held at bay,
　　His gallant men and bold.

Ready they are still to hold out,
　　And die, if so must be ;
Or sally forth with cry and shout
　　To meet the enemy.

But, as their cause was hopeless all,
　　He passed the castle gate,
And marched into the royal hall
　　Where the king did keep his state.

And then, with dauntless mien and word,
　　He looked John in the face,
And at his feet threw down his sword,
　　And asked for royal grace.

But, filled with wrath and rage, the king
　　By all the saints did say,
That he and all his men should swing
　　On gallows high that day.

Then up and spake Savarii bold—
　　Oh, but out and brave spake he—
" My lord the king, I pray you hold ;
　　This must not—shall not be !

" It were a base and coward thing
   To harm these soldiers brave ;
Unworthy of thee, noble king,
   To dig for them a grave !

" Nor is the war yet over, sire,
   Its fortunes soon may turn ;
The barons, filled with righteous ire,
   For vengeance fierce will burn.

" And if they conquer us in fight,
   Then *they* will work their will,
And will not spare a knave or knight,
   Will hang and burn and kill.

" And none will rise up in thy cause,
   No champion wilt thou find,
If thou dost break fair honour's laws,
   And cast them to the wind."

King John he heard with lowering look,
   With fierce and gleaming eyes ;
Such counsel he was loth to brook,
   Though he felt it true and wise.

And, after time of sullen gloom,
    The silence deep he broke,
And, with a brow as dark as doom,
    He to Savarii spoke.

D'Albiney and his men, he said,
    He should not hang, but spare ;
They to Corfe Castle should be led
    And kept in dungeon there.

And so it was. These men so bold,
    Baron, and Knave, and Knight,
Were in Corfe Castle placed in hold ;
    Maugre both ruth and right.

But God who watches o'er the brave,
    To rescue soon or late,
Let not the dungeon be their grave,
    Averting such a fate.

D'Albiney went across the main,
    And dwelt on foreign strand ;
Nor did he ever see again,
    His green and pleasant land.

A holy Monk of St. Alban's fair
  His body home did bring,
And laid it reverently where
  With hymns the cloisters ring.

In Wymondham, a saintly place,
  And blessed by priestly rite—
Wherever sound sweet songs of grace,
  And prayers rise day and night ;

They laid him with the chant and psalm,
  In a great and honoured tomb,
Where he lies in deep, untroubled calm,
  Till breaks the day of doom.

And to this shrine of the noble dead
  Full many a pilgrim stole,
To hear prayers read and masses said
  For the good D'Albiney's soul.

A LEGEND OF THE LAKES.

FAIR was she as an opening day,
　　Blushing with joy to find it May.

Sweet was she as some red June rose,
Ere all its crimson buds unclose.

Her hair was bright as ruddy morn,
In colour rich as the August corn.

Through a bosom fair as drifted snow,
Her gracious thoughts did come and go.

Her heart looked out of clear frank eyes,
Filled with all happy memories.

She was a noble Baron's child,
Who ruled o'er many a waste and wild,

And o'er broad acres rich and fair,
To which fair Hilda was sole heir.

Brother or sister she had none,
They died in early youth,—had gone

To that bright heav'n whose sapphire blue
Found in the lake a mirror true.

The Baron's castle darkly stood
Close to the waters, near a wood,

Through which there foamed with head-long course
The rapid streams of Ara Force ;

That rushed through many a bush and brake,
Till rest they found within the lake.

Here Hilda up to woman grew ;
Many her joys, her sorrows few.

She knew the great depths of the wood,
And where the ring-dove reared her brood ;

Where the first violet was found,
And rare long purples deck'd the ground ;

Where cuckoo-buds and harebells grew,
And purple fox-gloves held the dew.

Many a suiter sought her grace,
But in her heart none found a place :

The passions of their thrilling words
No music struck from love's sweet chords.

The same kind smile on all she bent,
Then on her way passed well content ;

As cold she seemed as Alpine snow
Without the Alpine rose's glow.

Sir Wilfrid woo'd her, loved her too,
As well as such a man could do ;

Loved her, but scarce as much as self :
Loved her, but also loved her pelf.

A man he was of craven soul,
Would win by means or fair or foul.

He woo'd and woo'd, but him she loathed,
Would rather death were her betrothed.

So she said " No," and " No," and " No,"
Yet paled before his look of woe.

But he was wroth, and nursed the ire
Which in his bosom burned like fire.

Came there at length a gallant knight,
Gentle in peace, and brave in fight,

With air like Michael's when he drew
His sword to smite the dragon through.

Sir Lyulph saw the maiden sweet,
Adored the ground beneath her feet;

Lived in the light of her clear eyes—
Her presence was like Paradise.

And she? Ah, now love's morning broke
O'er Memnon, and the music woke,

And thrilled and throbbed through every chord,
Till passions deepest depths were stirred.

His absence was delicious pain;
His presence sunshine after rain.

And as he spake the tender word,
Which all her quivering pulses stirred,

Low, earnest, truthful, as was meet,
Her trembling lips made answer sweet.

'Twas spring-time now; voluptuous June
Would bring them near their marriage moon.

The days were numbered as they passed,
And each was brighter than the last.

The Spring died out, and summer came,
And all the gardens were aflame.

Hedge-rows grew sweet with flowers fair,
That flung warm scents upon the air.

So days passed on; but now from far
Came summons to the holy war,

Waged by a brave and faithful band
To wrench from Turkish power the land

Where Christ the Saviour lived and died,
Was mocked, and scourged, and crucified.

And Lyulph, knight of grace, must go
To battle with the Paynim foe.

L

They parted, and fair Eden's gate
Seemed closed to leave them desolate.

Sir Wilfrid with Sir Lyulph went ;
Friends both in name, they shared one tent.

But Lyulph recked not of the dole
That strung to torture Wilfrid's soul,

Nor knew what evil things lurked there,
Beneath a face so bland and fair.

In many a bloody field they fought,
And many a deed of valour wrought ;

And side by side upon the plain
Left many a Paynim fooman slain.

But once, when Lyulph, over-bold,
Attacked the infidel in his hold,

Sir Wilfrid followed not, but there
Left him the battle's brunt to bear,

And hoped the avenging Turk might slay
Sir Lyulph in the bloody fray.

Back Lyulph came not : none could tell
If prisoner made, or if he fell

In combat slain—all knew him bold ;
If dead, that dear his life he sold.

The weeks went on, till ten months lay
Between that venture and the day

When Wilfrid, without page or state,
Came riding to the castle gate,

With troubled air, and all alone,
With sable plumes, on charger roan.

How could he his sad story tell
In Hilda's ears ?   It struck the knell

Of hope and love : of all, in sooth,
That lent a joy to her fair youth.

It smote her helpless to the ground,
And failed at once sense, sight, and sound.

Then came a dull and aching pain,
And then a wild unconscious brain,

And whirling words, all meaning gone,
Whilst reason tottered on her throne,

They placed her pale upon the bed,
She lay for days and days as dead.

But in the struggle life o'ercame,
She rose at length, but not the same.

A stricken thing in piteous case,
With great sad eyes and white wan face,

And the light step, that erst did go
Swift as a fawn's, grew dull and slow.

'Twas living death ; all hope was slain,
Would never bud or bloom again.

It now became her only joy,
And one that never seemed to cloy,

To sit and hear Sir Wilfrid's tale,
With weeping eyes and face all pale.

How Lyulph bore him in the fight,
His deeds of prowess and of might,

How he was first to storm the breach,
And fired his men by deeds and speech.

She listened well,—the widowed bride ;
And through her tears she flushed with pride

To hear of him, the true, the brave,
Who held her heart within his grave.

But most of all she loved to hear,
Often repeated in her ear,

His messages of love to her—
Then would her bosom throb and stir.

So Wilfrid gained upon her grace,
As looking daily in her face,

He told the story of her lord,
And deeds wrought by his valiant sword,

And how he saw her Lyulph die—
Heard his last words—received his sigh ;

And o'er his dying form bent low
To wipe the death-sweat from his brow.

And as she listened, listened still,
And knew her father's wish—his will,

She quelled the bitter inward strife,
And gave her word to be his wife ;

But yet she wept her woman's tears,
And trembled with her woman's fears,

As days did all too quickly glide
To that when at Sir Wilfrid's side

She would at holy altar stand,
And pledge her troth, and give her hand.

At length within the church they stood,
She in her young sweet womanhood ;

And oh, so fair—so wondrous fair,
In robe of silvery sheen—her hair,

With diamonds flashed, and pearls all white,
Lay on her breast like softened light.

Rich was his garb, as well became
A belted knight of warlike fame :

And in good sooth he seemed to be
True knight in grace and courtesy.

When the far-chiming bells had ceased,
In Mary's Chapel stood the priest,

A holy man, and old and grey,
And 'gan the solemn words to say.

But ere the troth-ring he had given,
And they were one in sight of Heaven,

There came a sudden hurried tread,
So loud, it might have waked the dead

Who slept, each in his shroud alone,
Beneath the sacred chancel stone.

A knight, all armed, strode up the aisle,
His helmet doff'd, and with a smile

That burned defiant, like a flame,
As on with steady pace he came ;

And then a stern deep voice was heard,
That through each bosom thrilled and stirred ;

" Hold, hold, Sir Priest, or by my faith,
Another word shall be thy death—

By promise, oath, and vow, and sign,
I claim this bride, for she is mine.

This perjured, forsworn, craven knight,
Like some foul ulcer hurts the sight.

False in deed, and false in word,
With him I deign to cross no sword.

Let him pass out through yonder gate,
Object of loathing and of hate."

Sir Wilfrid like an aspen shook,
With awe-struck eyes, and ashen look,

Half drew his sword from out its sheath,
Then paused with quick and labouring breath.

But Hilda, pale as some wan moon
That seems within night's arms to swoon,

Would down have fall'n upon the ground,
Had not her maidens gathered round,

And held her up a little space,
Clasped in their warm and fast embrace.

Out spoke the priest, and trembling said,
" Art living man, or from the dead ?

Who art thou ? Who ? On battle plain
Sir Lyulph lies amongst the slain.

This gallant knight did see him die,
And closed his eyes "—" Sir Priest, that lie

I thrust back in his throat,—his heart,
Ah ! craven soul ! thou well may'st start ;

A scorn and proverb be thy name,
Hence in thy self-contempt and shame ! "

He then with arms all opened wide,
Turned to the place where stood the bride,

And spoke : " Hilda, my love, my life,
I claim thee here my bride, my wife.

Say, am I not thine own,—thine own ?
Art thou not mine alone,—alone ?

Lo, in this holy place I stand,
Art thou not mine both heart and hand?

If thou art true, and lov'st me still,
Art here 'gainst heart, if not 'gainst will,

Come to this true and loving breast,
Here lay thy head down, love, and rest."

A cry through choir and chancel rang—
Into his folding arms she sprang,

And with a sense of joy and pain,
Felt her heart beat 'gainst his again.

All heaven seemed opened to them there,
Within that house of holy prayer.

Sir Wilfrid meantime shrunk away,
To hate and jealousy a prey;

A perjured, coward, selfish soul:
What was for him save bitter dole?

All good men's loathing, true men's scorn,
He passed forth friendless and forlorn.

Then Lyulph took the craven's place,
With Hilda in her pure, sweet grace—

And ere they left God's house of prayer,
The priest had blessed them kneeling there.

The words were said, the token given,
And they were one in sight of Heaven.

LINES FOR MUSIC.

THE leaves have been whisp'ring all the day,
    They are trembling still in the air;
And I think I can guess what they wish to say,
    What message to me they bear.

For my darling has been in the wood, I know,
    By the way we used often to pass,
And the little foot that is whiter than snow,
    Has brushed the dews from the grass.

And if leaves could speak they would tell me this,
    That she leaned here tenderly,
And plucking a flower she gave it a kiss,
    And told it her love for me.

And she called me her own, her own, her own,
    And she said it again and again;
For her heart I know is a happy throne,
    Where lord of her love I reign.

Ah leaves, dear leaves, that tremble and thrill
   When woo'd by the summer wind,
Your whispers my soul with a rapture fill,
   My heart with their spell they bind.

Oh tell her, sweet leaves, when she comes this way,
   And rests 'neath your happy tree,
That I love her—oh, better than words can say,
   That she's all in all to me.

And tell her, oh tell her, my love, my life,
   So close to my heart she lies,
That the day I call her my bride, my wife,
   Will turn earth to Paradise.

PRINTED BY BALLANTYNE, HANSON AND CO.
EDINBURGH AND LONDON